Abraham Coles

Latin Hymns

With Original Translations

Abraham Coles

Latin Hymns
With Original Translations

ISBN/EAN: 9783744779142

Printed in Europe, USA, Canada, Australia, Japan

Cover: Foto ©Andreas Hilbeck / pixelio.de

More available books at **www.hansebooks.com**

 Latin Hymns

WITH

ORIGINAL TRANSLATIONS

IN FOUR PARTS

I. DIES IRÆ (In Thirteen Versions)
II. STABAT MATER (DOLOROSA)
III. STABAT MATER (SPECIOSA)
IV. OLD GEMS IN NEW SETTINGS

BY

ABRAHAM COLES, M. D., LL. D.

ILLUSTRATED

NEW YORK
D. APPLETON AND COMPANY
1892

NEWARK, N. J.
ADVERTISER PRINTING HOUSE,
1892

DIES IRÆ.

DESCRIPTION OF THE FRONTISPIECE.

THE "Dies Iræ" of painting by the greateſt of painters, Michel Angelo's famous fresco of the *Laſt Judgment*, confeſſedly the moſt extraordinary picture in the
hiſtory of Art, occupies the end wall of the Siſtine Chapel at
Rome, and is forty-five feet wide by fifty-seven feet high.
It was completed and firſt thrown open to the public on
Chriſtmas Day, 1546. The artiſt was then in his sixty-
seventh year, and had been employed on the paintings and
cartoons nearly nine years. "We have seen," says one,
"Michel Angelo, and he is terrible." In the centre of this
vaſt compoſition, confiſting of at leaſt two hundred figures in
every conceivable attitude, appears the majeſtic form of the
Saviour in the act of pronouncing sentence upon the wicked,
"Depart," etc. By his ſide is the Virgin. Near her, towards the right, is a figure with the back turned, done in the
ſtyle of the fineſt antique; and next beyond is Adam, ex-
preſſing by the contour of his members and his relaxed
muscles extreme old age. Between these two, half-way
down, can be seen a face, with long flowing beard, answering to our idea of an ancient patriarch. Farther to the
right is a woman, defigned with exquiſite grace and elegance, with a young girl clinging to her and hiding her face
in terror. On the left of the Saviour, the ſtooping figure is
Peter, in the act of surrendering the keys; the face cloſe to
his is Moses. The group behind represents the prophets in
ſtudied and ſtriking attitudes. Below are the martyrs, with
the symbols of their sufferings. Juſt at the feet of the Virgin is St. Lawrence, with his gridiron (*la graticola*); then
comes St. Bartholomew, with a knife in one hand and his
ſkin in the other; St. Catharine is known by her broken
wheel; St. Hippolytus, by his currycombs with iron teeth;
St. Sebaſtian, by his arrows held in his left hand. Higher up
is St. Andrew on a cross, a fine figure. Above and around
is an innumerable company of the bleſſed. In the angles at

DESCRIPTION OF THE FRONTISPIECE.

the higheſt part are angels, bearing, on one ſide, the cross, the crown of thorns, the dice used in caſting lots on Chriſt's garment; and on the other, the pillar of scourging, etc. Far below is another group of angels, blowing seven trumpets to wake the dead, two of them holding in their hands the books of life and death. At the right, near the bottom, are seen the dead in all ſtages of decay, quickened and ſlowly riſing,—saints and angels aſſiſting the righteous in their ascent to heaven. In one case a demon makes conteſt for poſſeſſion. On the left is presented the terrific spectacle of the condemned dragged down by demons,—among them, a wicked pope, with the keys in his hand, falling headlong the prey of exultant fiends; also a licentious cardinal, a living contemporary of the artiſt. "Forms and faces," says one, "more trembling and convulsed with despair were never embodied or conceived." Charon, the infernal ferryman, in accordance with Dante's description,—

> "With eyes of burning coal, collects them all,
> Beckoning, and each that lingers with his oar
> Strikes." *Inferno*, Canto iii. vv. 102–104.

In the extreme left corner, at the loweſt point, are two heads, "one a cowl unto the other," borrowed likewise from Dante,—Count Ugolino gnawing the ſkull of his enemy:—

> "Upon the wretched ſkull his teeth
> He faſtened, like a maſtiff's, 'gainſt the bone
> Firm and unyielding."
> *Inferno*, Canto xxxiii. vv. 74–76.

Close by is Midas, with aſſ's ears and serpent around the body,—a likeness of, it is said, and a savage satire upon, Meſſer Biaggio, his critic. At the foot of the picture, in the middle, is the pit of hell, with demons at its mouth.—The miniature copy here given, photographed from an outline engraving by Piroli, firſt publiſhed at Paris in 1808, faithful and full, down to the minuteſt anatomical details, was deemed not an inappropriate embelliſhment to this volume. If deſired, it can be indefinitely magnified by a glass.

IN

THIRTEEN ORIGINAL VERSIONS

BY

ABRAHAM COLES, M. D., Ph. D.

SIXTH EDITION.

NEW YORK

D. APPLETON AND COMPANY

1891

ILLUSTRATIONS.

———◆———

DIES IRÆ.

Last Judgment.   (M. Angelo — Rubens — Cornelius).
> O what fear shall it engender,
> When the Judge shall come in splendor,
> Strict to mark and just to render !

Christus Remunerator.   (Ary Scheffer.)
> Be there, Lord, my place decided,
> With Thy sheep from goats divided,
> Kindly to Thy right hand guided !

STABAT MATER (DOLOROSA).

Mary at the Cross.   (Carlo Dolce — Paul Delaroche).
> Stood th' afflicted mother weeping,
> Near the cross her station keeping,
> Whereon hung her Son and Lord.

STABAT MATER (SPECIOSA).

Nativity.   LA NOTTE.   (Correggio).

Virgin and Child.   MADONNA DI SAN SISTO.   (Raphael.)
> Oh what grace to her allotted,
> Blessèd mother and unspotted
>> Of the Sole Begotten One !

OLD GEMS IN NEW SETTINGS

> O country most dear, our longing eyes here
> As they view thee afar with desire are aching.

> My innermost eyes, thus piercing the skies,
> From the mind's highest peaks delighted behold thee.
>
> . . . .
>
> Now in thee I am glad, now in me I am sad,
> I sob and I sigh with breast heaving and swelling.

INTRODUCTION.

T would be difficult to find, in the whole range of literature, a production to which a profounder intereſt attaches than to that magnificent canticle of the Middle Ages, the DIES IRÆ. Faſtening on that which is indeſtructible in man, and giving fitter expreſſion than can elsewhere be found, to experiences and emotions which can never cease to agitate him, it has loſt after the lapse of ſix centuries none of its original freſhness and transcendent power to affect the heart. It has commanded alike the admiration of men of piety and men of taſte. By common consent, it is as Daniel remarks: *sacræ poeseos summum decus et Ecclesiæ Latinæ κειμήλιον est pretioſiſſimum.* Among gems it is the diamond. It is solitary in

ts excellence. Of Latin Hymns, it is the beſt known and the acknowledged maſterpiece. There are others which poſſeſs much sweetness and beauty, but this ſtands unrivalled. It has superior beauties, with none of their defeᴄts. For the moſt part they are more or less Romiſh, but this is Catholic, and not Romiſh at all. It is universal as humanity. It is the cry of the human. It bears indubitable marks of being a personal experience.

The author is supposed to have been a monk: an incredible suppoſition truly did we not know that a monk is also a man. One thing is certain, that the monk does not appear, and that it is the man only that speaks. He no longer dreams and drivels. He is effeᴄtually awake. The veil is lifted. He sees Chriſt coming to Judgment. All the tumult and the terror of the Laſt Day are present to him. The final pause and syncope of Nature ; the ſhuddering of a horror-ſtruck Universe ; the down-ruſhing and wreck of all things—all are present. But these material circumſtances of horror and amazement, he feels are as nothing compared with " the infinite terror of being found guilty before the Juſt Judge." This fingle confideration swallows up every other. The interefts of an eternity are crowded into a moment.

One great fecret of the power and enduring popularity of this Hymn is, undoubtedly, its genuineness. A vital fincerity breathes throughout. It is a cry *de profundis ;* and the cry becomes sometimes—so intense are the terror and solicitude—almoft a fhriek. It is in the higheft degree pathetic. The Muse is " Mater Lachrymarum, Our Lady of Tears." Every line weeps. Underneath every word and syllable, a living heart throbs and pulsates. The very rhythm, or that alternate elevation and depreffion of the voice, which prosodifts call the *arfis* and the *thefis*, one might almoft fancy were synchronous with the contraction and the dilatation of the heart. It is more than dramatic. The horror and the dread are real : are actual not acted. A human heart is laid bare, quivering with life, and we see and hear its tumultuous throbbings. We sympathize—nay, before we are aware, we have changed places. We, too, tremble and quail and cry aloud.

All true Lyric Poetry is subjective. The DIES IRÆ is, as we have seen, remarkable for its intense

subjectivity ; and whoever duly appreciates this characteriftic, will have little difficulty in underftanding
its superior effectiveness over everything else that
has been written on the same theme. The life of
the writer has paffed into it and informs it, so that it
is itself alive. It has vital forces and emanations.
Its life mingles with our life. It enters into our
veins and circulates in our blood. A virtue goes out
from it. It is electrically charged, and contact is
inftantly followed by a fhock and fhuddering.

Springing from its subjectivity, if not identical with
it, we would further notice, the intenfifying effect of
what may be called its personalism, in other words
its ego-ism. It is I and not We. Subftitute the
plural pronoun for the fingular, and it would lose
half its pungency. We have had occafion to observe
the weakening effect of this in tranflation. The
truth is, the feeling is of a kind too concentrated and
too exacting to allow itself to be diffipated in the
vagueness of any grouping generality. The heart
knoweth its own bitterness. There is a grief that
cannot be fhared, neither can it be joined on to
another's. It is not social nor common. It is mine

and not yours. It is excluſive, not because it is sel-
fish, but because it has depths beyond the soundings
of ordinary sympathy.

This is especially true of some of the intenser
forms of religious experience, proceeding as they do
from that which is moſt intimate and innermoſt, the
penetralia of a man's consciousness, his moſt secret
and peculiar self. There is an inner and privileged
sanctuary of the heart, which is kept as a chamber
locked up. It is hidden and sacred. It may be,
that the individual, dwelling habitually in the outer
courts of his being, rarely if ever enters into it himself. For man is twofold. A veil divides between
the outer and the inner man. Gross and sensual,
the majority of mankind are averse to lifting the con-
cealing medium, for fear of unwelcome revelations
and discoveries respecting themselves. Goethe is an
example of this portentous preference for half knowledge : " Man," he says, " is a darkened being ; he
knows not whence he came, nor whither he goes ;
he knows little of the world and less of himself. I
know not myself, and may God protect me from it."

In converſion to God this veil is rent from top to

bottom. There is a self-revelation. Behind the curtain, there in the Moſt Holy Place, where ought to be the Shekinah, the ſhining, senſible Manifeſtation of the Divine Preſence, he beholds the Abomination of Iniquity set up. He awakes to the ſtartling fact that he is " without God and without hope in the world." A voice of urgency is sounding in his ears : "Flee from the Wrath to Come." He anticipates the terrors of the Judgment. He feels that there is not a moment to lose. Instinct prompts, and the Word of God enjoins, that he seek to save himself firſt. He knows not whether others are in as bad a caſe as he. But of his own guilt and danger he has no doubt. An offended Maker confronts him, him in particular. So he prays and agonizes. His may not be " the thews which throw the world"—he is conscious of weakness rather than ſtrength—yet ſingly and alone, he wreſtles with God like Jacob, and prevails like Israel.

The Hymn is not only lyrical in its eſſence, but also in its form. It is inſtinct with muſic. It ſings itself. The grandeur of its rhythm, and the aſſonance and chime of its fit and powerful words, are, even in the ears of those unacquainted with the Latin language, suggeftive of the richeft and mightieft harmonies. The verse is ternary; and the ternary number, having been efteemed anciently a symbol of perfection and held in great veneration, may possibly have had something to do with the choice of the ftrophe. Be this as it may, its metrical ftructure, as all agree, conftitutes by no means the leaft of its extraordinary merits. Trench, in his Selections from Latin Poetry, speaks of the metre as being grandly devised, and fitted to bring out some of the nobleft powers of the Latin language; and as being, moreover, unique, forming the only example of the kind that he remembers. He notices the solemn effect of the triple rhyme, comparable to blow following blow of the hammer on the anvil. Knapp, in his Liederschatz, likens the original to a blaft from the trump of resurrection, and declares its power inimitable in any tranflation.

HISTORY OF THE HYMN.

HE authorſhip of the Dies Iræ is as-
cribed, apparently upon good grounds,
to Thomas of Celano, so called from a
small town of that name in Italy. He
was a friend and pupil and subsequently the biographer of St. Francis of Aſſiſi, the founder of the
order of Minorites, (called also Friars-Minor, Grey
Friars or Franciscans, being one of the four orders
of mendicant friars,) inſtituted in 1208. Wadding,
an Iriſhman and a Minorite, who lived in the firſt
half of the seventeenth century, and who wrote a
hiſtory of his order, expreſſly refers it to Celano.
He mentions two other hymns or Sequences composed by him, one beginning: *Fregit viĉtor virtua-
lis*; the other: *Sanĉtitatis nova ſigna*. The circum-

ftance of the Dominican Sixtus Senenfis affecting
to sneer at it, calling it *rhythmus inconditus*, is regarded as confirmatory of the opinion, that it was at
leaft the work of a Franciscan; the bitter rivalries
subfifting between the two orders affording, it is
thought, the moft plaufible explanation of a criticism
so manifeftly splenetic and unjuft. Another cor-
roborative circumftance is its early admiffion into
the Franciscan Miffals, by which means a knowledge of it was spread throughout Europe. The
correctness of this inference is further suftained by
the fact, that, inscribed on a marble flab in the
Franciscan Church of St. Francis at Mantua, was
found one of the earlieft copies of the hymn, representing, it is believed, the text as it came from
the hands of the author. Dr. Mohnike, a learned
and able editor of the Dies Iræ, furnifhes an old
copy of the Mantuan text, which differs from the
Received Text chiefly in this, that the firft four
ftanzas are additional. They are here given with
a tranflation annexed; also the heading which is as
follows :

Meditatio Vetufta et Venufta
   de Noviffimo Judicio
quæ Mantuæ in æde D. Francisci in
   marmore legitur.

1. Cogita, anima fidelis,
   Ad quid respondere velis,
   Chrifto venturo de cœlis.

     Weigh with solemn thought and tender,
     What response, thou, Soul, wilt render,
     Then when Chrift fhall come in splendor

2. Cum deposcet rationem
   Ob boni omiffionem,
   Ob mali commiffionem.

     And thy life fhall be inspected,
     All its hidden guilt detected,
     Evil done and good neglected.

3. Dies illa, dies iræ,
   Quam conemur prævenire
   Obviamque Deo ire;

     For that day of vengeance neareth
     Ready be each one that heareth
     God to meet when He appeareth.

4.   Seria contritione,
      Gratiæ apprehenfione,
      Vitæ emendatione.

         By repenting, by believing,
         By God's offered grace receiving,
         By all evil courfes leaving.

The succeeding fixteen verfes are the same, with
flight variations, as those of the Church or Received
text; but in place of the next verse, which forms
the 17th of this, beginning: *Oro supplex et acclinis*,
the Mantuan copy has the following for its 21ft and
concluding ftanza:

21.   Confors ut beatitatis
       Vivam cum juftificatis
       In ævum æternitatis. Amen.

         That in fellowfhip fraternal
         With inhabitants supernal
         I may live the life eternal. Amen.

That the abbreviation of the poem, by the omis-
fion of the four opening ftanzas, adds greatly to its
general, and ftill more to its lyric effectiveness, there
can be no doubt. The rejected verfes, partaking of

a quiet and meditative character, impair the force of
the lyric element. In its present form, all is vehe-
ment ftir and movement, from the grand and ftart-
ling abruptness of its opening, to the sweet and
powerful pathos of its solemn and impreffive close.

Befides Celano, various other names have had
their supporters for the honor of the authorfhip of
this poem. It has been attributed to Gregory the
Great, who lived at a period some fix hundred
years earlier. But this would involve the neceffity
of suppofing that a poem of such extraordinary merit
could remain unknown and unnoticed during so
many centuries, which is not at all likely. Befides,
it is certain, that, while rhyme was not altogether
unknown or unused at that time, it had by no means
reached that ftate of perfection which this poem
exhibits.*

Leonard Meifter, a Swiss writer, claimed that
Felix Hämmerlin, (Latinized into Malleolus,) a
Church dignitary of Zürich, born in 1389, and who
died about 1457, was the author of Dies Iræ, because
among Hämmerlin's poems he found a manuscript
of this hymn ; but the evidence is quite conclufive,

* See Appendix—Origin of Latin Rhyme.

c

that the hymn was in exiſtence before his time. In
the Hämmerlin text, the 16th verse is followed by
eight more, probably supplied by Hämmerlin himself. They are here subjoined.

17.   Oro supplex a ruinis,
        Cor contritum quaſi cinis:
        Gere curam mei finis!

           From the ruins of creation,
             Make I contrite supplication:
             Interpose for my salvation!

18.   Lachrymosa die illa,
        Cum resurget ex favilla,
        Tanquam ignis ex scintilla,

           On that day of woe and weeping,
             When, like fire from spark upleaping,
             Starts, from aſhes where he's ſleeping.

19.   Judicandus homo reus,
        Huic ergo parce, Deus!
        Eſto semper adjutor meus!

           Man account to Thee to render:
             Spare the miserable offender!
             Be my Helper and Defender!

20.   Quando cœli sunt movendi,
      Dies adsunt tunc tremendi,
      Nullum tempus pœnitendi.

          When the heavens away are flying,
          Days of trembling then and crying,
          For repentance time denying;

21.   Sed salvatis læta dies,
      Et damnatis nulla quies,
      Sed dæmonum effigies.

          To the saved a day of gladness,
          To the damned a day of sadness,
          Demon forms and shapes of madness.

22.   O tu Deus majeftatis,
      Alme candor Trinitatis,
      Nunc conjunge cum beatis!

          God of infinite perfection,
          Trinity's serene reflection,
          Give me part with the election!

23.   Vitam meam fac felicem
      Propter tuam genetricem,
      Jeffe florem et radicem.

Happiness upon me fhower,
For Thy Mother's sake, with power
Who is Jeffe's root and flower.

24.   Præfta nobis tunc levamen,
Dulce noftrum fac certamen,
Ut clamemus omnes, Amen !

From Thy fulness comfort pour us,
Fight Thou with us or fight for us,
So we'll fhout, Amen, in chorus.

Taking for granted that the Mantuan was the original text, it would follow that the truncation of the four introductory verfes spoken of had already taken place at the time of Hämmerlin; and it is furthermore obvious that the 17th and 18th verfes of the Received Text muft have been formed out of the firft three of the supplemented verfes of Hämmerlin, as follows, viz. : by subftituting, in the 17th verfe, " et acclinis " for " a ruinis," and taking the firft two lines of the two succeeding verfes, being triplets, to make up the 18th verse, which confifts of four lines. Bating a few verbal variations, the firft fixteen verfes of the Hämmerlin and

Church texts correspond. The laſt named is founded on the Roman Miſſal firſt publiſhed in 1567, under the sanction and after the reviſion of the Council of Trent. It forms the baſis of the present, as it does of moſt tranſlations.

A brief reference to some of the more important variations in the text, and an explanation of certain alluſions which occur therein, may not be unintereſt-ing. The firſt line, *Dies iræ, dies illa*, plainly points to a paſſage of Scripture from the Vulgate,— Zephaniah I. 15. The whole verse reads thus : " DIES IRÆ, DIES ILLA, dies tribulationis et anguſtiæ, dies calamitatis et miseriæ, dies tenebrarum et caligi-nis, dies nebulæ et turbinis, dies tubæ et clangoris." In the third line, the change of the Mantuan read-ing, " Petro " into " David," as it now ſtands, may have been due, it is conjectured, to a feeling that there was greater appropriateness in David's being aſſociated with the ante-Chriſtian Sibyl. From the averſion felt to the introduction of a heathen Sibyl into a Chriſtian and ſtill more a Church hymn, a Miſſal of the diocese of Metz, publiſhed in 1778, rejecting the third line, adopts, but without

the authority of a single manuscript, another reading
as follows :

> Dies iræ, dies illa,
> Crucis expandens vexilla,
> Solvet sæclum in favilla.

> Day of wrath, that day amazing,
> High the bannered cross upraising,
> While the universe is blazing.

The allusion here is to the sign of the coming of
the Son of Man in heaven, mentioned in Matthew
xxiv. 3 ; and is indicative of the belief, that the sign
there spoken of would have its fulfilment in the
apparition of a cross in the sky.   But the older and
the true reading is doubtless the other, which refers
to the Sibyl as bearing concurrent testimony with
the prophet of the Old or the New Testament,
David or Peter, (Psalm xcvi. 13 ; xcvii. 3 ; xi.
6 ; 2 Peter iii. 7,) touching the destruction of the
world and the final judgment.   The 2d, 7th, and 8th
books of the " Sibylline Oracles " are full of passages which refer to these, but it is probable that the
reference here is more immediately to verses ex-

tracted therefrom, found in Lactantius (Divin. In-
ftitut. lib. vii. De Vita Beata, cap. 16–24). In the
earlier ages of the Church, these pretended prophecies
were regarded with no little veneration ; wherefore
it is by no means uncommon to find Chriftian writers placing them fide by fide with Scriptural prophecies, and, as in the case before us, making solemn
appeal to them. The discovery of their true character as worthless forgeries was reserved for a later
period.

This poem, which, there is every reason to believe,
was originally the inspiration of retirement, the solitary outpouring of

> "a suppliant heart all crufhed
> And crumbled into contrite duft,"—

to adopt the language of Crafhaw's verfion at the 17th
verse,—came afterwards, when it had paffed into
Church use, to receive the title of SEQUENCE, from
the place affigned to it in the service of the Mass
for the Dead. The precise time when this occurred
cannot be determined, but it muft have been early,
for Albizzi speaks of it as being in common use
as a Sequence in 1385. For an explanation of this

term, the reader is referred to the Appendix at the end of this volume.

If the origin of the hymn be somewhat obscure, not so have been its subsequent fortunes. Through the long centuries that have elapsed fince the time it firft became known to the world, its extraordinary merits have been fteadily recognized. Its light has been that of a ftar, whose keen and diamond luftre intermits not nor grows dim, but fhines on the same from age to age. Its miffion from the beginning has been one of power. To some, there is reason to believe, it has been "the power of God unto salvation." Scattered everywhere along its track are seen the luminous footprints of its victorious progress as the subduer of hearts. The greateft minds have delighted to bear teftimony to its worth. Goethe evinced his appreciation of it by introducing certain verses of it into his "Fauft,"—with how grand an effect we all know. Boswell relates of Dr. Johnson, that, "when he would try to repeat the celebrated *Prosa Ecclefiaftica pro Mortuis*, beginning : *Dies iræ, dies illa*, he could never pass the ftanza ending thus : *Tantus labor non fit caffus*, without burfting into a flood of tears."

It is said that Ancina, a Profeſſor of Medicine in the Univerſity of Turin, was so ſtrongly affected by hearing one day the Dies Iræ chanted in the service for the dead, that he determined to abandon the world.   He afterwards became Biſhop of Saluzzo. Milman, in his " Hiſtory of Chriſtianity," speaking of the Latin poetry of the Chriſtian Church, remarks : " There is nothing, in my judgment, to be compared with the monkiſh *Dies iræ, dies illa.*"   To these names might be added those of many other eminent scholars and critics, all bearing like teſtimony.   But the crowning proof of its unrivalled excellence is found in the fact, that, mingled with the ſighs and gaspings of diſſolving Nature, the measured beat of its melodious rhythm has been so often heard ; now, it may be, in the soft murmur of words half audible, and now in the clear tones of a diſtinct utterance, iſſuing from the pale and trembling lips of the dying. The Earl of Roscommon, we are told, repeated with great energy and devotion, in the moment when he expired, two lines of his own tranſlation of the 17th verse :—

    " My God, my Father, and my Friend,
      Do not forsake me in my end!"

d

Sir Walter Scott evinced his regard for it in the same affecting manner, during his laft hours : " We very often," says his biographer, " heard diftinctly the cadence of the Dies Iræ."

It is certainly somewhat remarkable, that, while thus solemnly affociated with the dying moments of these two illuftrious mafters of song, who had likewise employed their pens in the tafk of rendering it into Englifh, it fhould have had a connection not diffimilar with the death of that great composer by whose means this immortal poem has come to be worthily wedded to immortal mufic.   It is well known that Mozart's Requiem is founded on it.   This, his greateft work, perhaps, was deftined also to be his laft, of which, it is said, he had a solemn presentiment.   His death occurred before it was entirely finifhed.   Befides Mozart, other diftinguifhed composers, such as Cherubini, Haydn, Jomelli, Paläftrina, and Pergolefi, have exercised their genius upon the same theme and the same text.

TRANSLATIONS OF THE HYMN.

THE number of tranflations made of this hymn into different languages it were not easy to eftimate. Those in German are particularly numerous. In a work dedicated to these, edited by Dr. F. G. Lisco, (Berlin, 1840,) as many as seventy verfions, more or less complete, arc given; the number being further increased three years afterwards by the addition of seventeen others, appended to a volume of tranflations, by the same editor, of the Stabat Mater.*

* For the loan of both the above works the writer is indebted to the Rev. William R. Williams, D. D., who, in a Note, afterwards somewhat enlarged and thrown into an Appendix, affixed to an Address on the " Confervative Principle of our Literature," firft publifhed in 1843, and subsequently included in his volume of " Miscellanies," has, with his usual

There is one in French, one in Romaic or Modern Greek, one in Dutch, and one in Latin, all the rest being German. In nearly every case, pains have been taken to preserve the exact measure and form of the original. The superior flexibility of the German, and its greater supply of words adapted for double rhyme, give tranflators in that language a decided advantage. The difficulty involved in triplicating the double rhymes, owing to the poverty of our language in words suitable for the purpose, without practifing awkward and inelegant inverfions, is probably the reason why English tranflators, even where they have been careful to retain the triplet form of the ftanza, have failed to preserve the rhyming close.

Crafhaw's, one of the oldeft and nobleft of the English tranflations, and which in the opinion of an eminent critic was not surpaffed by anything he ever wrote, is done in quatrains, or fingle rhymed couplets

eloquence and exhauftive learning, given a very full and inftructive account of this hymn and its tranflations ; adding in the later editions a verfion of his own, one of the first made in ternary double rhyme.

repeated ; and, on account of the freeness of the rendering, might more properly be called a reproduction
than a tranflation.   The Earl of Roscommon, celebrated in Dryden's verse as the greateft poet of his
time, was the author of a verfion praised by Pope
as the beft of his poetical performances ; although he
is confidered as having borrowed both from Crafhaw
and Dryden.   It is in triplets like the original, but
without double rhyme, and the verse is iambic inftead of trochaic.

The few verfes introduced by Sir Walter Scott
into the " Lay of the Laft Minftrel," and which have
found their way into almoft all the more recent Col-
lections of Hymns used in our Churches, though
spirited and impreffive, can scarcely be called a translation, being little more than an echo of one or two
of the leading sentiments of the Latin original.
Another familiar hymn, contained in moft Hymn
books, commencing,

> " Lo ! He comes in clouds descending,"

purports to be a tranflation of the Dies Iræ ; but
in respect neither to form nor spirit does it corre-

spond very accurately to the original. Although there
are other verfions of more or less merit, some made
by our own scholars, a further enumeration might be
tedious. "It is not wonderful," as Trench remarks,
"that a poem such as this fhould have continually
allured and continually defied tranflators."

The Author of the Tranflations here publifhed
scarcely knows how to fhield himself from the im-
putation of presumption to which his attempt exposes him. The number of his verfions is Thirteen. The first fix have the somewhat rare merit,
so far at leaft as Englifh verfions are concerned, of
being metrically conformed, both as it respects
rhyme and rhythm, to the original. The five succeeding ones are like in rhythm, but vary from the
original in not preserving the double rhyme. The
one which follows is in iambic triplets, like Roscommon's; and the laft in quatrains, after the manner
of Crafhaw's verfion.

It has been the aim of the Tranflator to be in all
cafes as faithful as poffible to the senfe and spirit
of the original, and likewise to the letter, but not
so flavifhly as to preclude variety. He has en-

deavored to carry out likeness in unlikeness, and to give to each verſion, so far as practicable, the intereſt of a diſtinct poem. How far he has succeeded others muſt judge. The preservation of the double rhyme involved some special difficulties, which he has overcome as well as he could ; but he would not be surprised if some readers preferred the eaſier metres, and indulges the hope that the multiplication of verſions may serve, among other things, to meet this diverſity of taſte. But there are some, if he mistakes not, who enjoy those pleasing surprises in viewing an object, that result from an altered attitude and a new angle of vision,—the curious changes which follow every fresh turn of a revolving kaleidoscope,—and the writer is willing therefore to believe that such, at any rate, will not be displeased at this attempt to supply the deficiency of one verſion by another and yet another, in the hope that thereby the original may be exhibited, approximately at least, in its solid entireness.

Young, in his " Eſſay on Lyric Poetry," aſſerts that difficulty overcome gives grace and pleasure, and he accounts for the pleasure of rhyme in general

upon this principle.   Having failed in his own case
to afford an exemplification of great success in this
particular, his critic and biographer, Johnson, somewhat sarcastically remarks: " But then the writer
must take care that the difficulty is overcome ; that
is, he must make rhyme consist with as perfect
sense and expression as would be expected, if he
were perfectly free from that shackle."   Hence, the
greater the difficulties to be surmounted, the greater
is the need of elaboration, until art conceals art.

The present Translator, recognizing fully the pro-
priety of the rule here stated, does not feel that he
has any right to plead the arduousness of his task, as
an excuse for any instances, if such there be, of
forced and unnatural construction, resorted to in
order to meet the exigencies of rhyme or metre.
What is called poetic license is, he is aware, a
license of power and grace, and not of weakness and
deformity, being tantamount to a license to dance or
sing, in place of ordinary walking or speaking.   Poetic chains, undoubtedly, were meant not to confine
and cripple, but to regulate movement in conformity
with settled laws ; the object being, not to punish

speech, but to exalt and honor it,—to grace language, not disgrace it.

To preserve, in connection with the utmost fidelity and ftrictness of rendering, all the rhythmic merits of the Latin original,—to attain to a vital likeness as well as to an exact literalness, at the same time that nothing is sacrificed of its mufical sonorousness and billowy grandeur, easy and graceful in its swing as the ocean on its bed,—to make the verbal copy, otherwise cold and dead, glow with the fire of lyric passion,—to reflect, and that too by means of a fingle verfion, the manifold aspects of the many-sided original, exhaufting at once its wonderful fulness and pregnancy,—to cause the white light of the primitive so to pass through the medium of another language as that it fhall undergo no refraction whatever,— would be defirable, certainly, were it practicable; but so much as this it were unreasonable to expect in any tranflation.

All the verfions here given were written and nearly ready for the press more than two years ago; but, influenced partly by a senfe of their imperfectness, and partly by a doubt as to the reception that a book

e

excluſively devoted to a ſingle hymn might meet with from the public, the Translator has delayed their appearance until now, when, encouraged by the favorable opinion expreſſed by some, whoſe names, were it proper to give them, would be re-garded, he doubts not, as an apology for his bold-ness, he ventures the experiment of publication. He does not deny that the amount of public favor that has been already accorded to two of the ver-ſions, viz., those marked I. and II., publiſhed anony-mouſly in the "Newark Daily Advertiser" sev-eral years ſince, the firſt as long ago as 1847, has had something to do with overcoming his diſtruſt. To avoid misapprehenſion, it is right to ſtate, that two verses of the firſt were introduced into Mrs. Stowe's "Uncle Tom's Cabin," and by these acci-dental means have enjoyed a world-wide currency. More recently this verſion has been honored with a place in the "Plymouth Collection of Hymns and Tunes," edited by Henry Ward Beecher, and ſet to muſic. It was, so far as the Tranſlator knows, the firſt attempt, with a ſingle exception, to repro-duce in English the ternary double rhyme of the original.

DIES iræ, dies illa
Solvet sæclum in favillâ,
Teſte David cum Sibyllâ.

Quantus tremor eſt futurus,
Quando Judex eſt venturus,
Cuncta ſtrictè discuſſurus!

Tuba, mirum spargens sonum
Per sepulchra regionum,
Coget omnes ante thronum.

Mors ſtupebit et natura,
Quum resurget creatura
Judicanti responsura.

1

Liber scriptus proferetur,
In quo totum continetur,
De quo mundus judicetur.

Judex ergo quum sedebit,
Quidquid latet, apparebit,
Nil inultum remanebit.

Quod sum miser tunc dicturus,
Quem patronum rogaturus,
Quum vix juſtus ſit securus?

Rex tremendæ majeſtatis,
Qui salvandos salvas gratis,
Salva me, fons pietatis!

Recordare, Jesu pie,
Quod sum causa tuæ viæ,
Ne me perdas illâ die!

Quærens me sediſti laſſus,
Redemiſti crucem paſſus:
Tantus labor non ſit caſſus!

Jufte Judex ultionis,
Donum fac remiffionis
Ante diem rationis!

Ingemisco tanquam reus,
Culpâ rubet vultus meus :
Supplicanti parce, Deus!

Qui Mariam absolvifti,
Et latronem exaudifti,
Mihi quoque spem dedifti.

Præces meæ non sunt dignæ,
Sed tu bonus fac benignè
Ne perenni cremer igne!

Inter oves locum præfta,
Et ab hædis me sequeftra,
Statuens in parte dextrâ!

Confutatis maledictis,
Flammis acribus addictis,
Voca me cum benedictis!

Oro supplex et acclinis,
Cor contritum quasi cinis :
Gere curam mei finis !

Lachrymosa dies illa,
Qua resurget ex favillâ,
Judicandus homo reus :
Huic ergo parce, Deus !

I.

AY of wrath, that day of burning,
Seer and Sibyl speak concerning,
All the world to afhes turning.

Oh, what fear fhall it engender,
When the Judge fhall come in splendor,
Strict to mark and juft to render !

Trumpet, scattering sounds of wonder,
Rending sepulchres asunder,
Shall resiftless summons thunder.

All aghaft then Death fhall fhiver,
And great Nature's frame fhall quiver,
When the graves their dead deliver.

Volume, from which nothing's blotted,
Evil done nor evil plotted,
Shall be brought and dooms allotted.

When ſhall ſit the Judge unerring,
He'll unfold all here occurring,
Vengeance then no more deferring.

What ſhall *I* say, that time pending?
Ask what advocate's befriending,
When the juſt man needs defending?

Dreadful King, all power poſſeſſing,
Saving freely those confeſſing,
Save thou me, O Fount of Bleſſing!

Think, O Jesus, for what reason
'Thou didſt bear earth's spite and treason,
Nor me lose in that dread season!

Seeking me Thy worn feet haſted,
On the cross Thy soul death taſted:
Let such travail not be waſted!

Righteous Judge of retribution !
Make me gift of absolution
Ere that day of execution !

Culprit-like, I plead, heart-broken,
On my cheek fhame's crimson token :
Let the pardoning word be spoken !

Thou, who Mary gav'ft remiffion,
Heard'ft the dying Thief's petition,
Cheer'ft with hope my loft condition.

Though my prayers be void of merit,
What is needful, Thou confer it,
Left I endless fire inherit !

Be there, Lord, my place decided
With Thy fheep, from goats divided,
Kindly to Thy right hand guided !

When th' accursed away are driven,
To eternal burnings given,
Call me with the blessed to heaven !

I beseech Thee, proſtrate lying,
Heart as aſhes, contrite, ſighing,
Care for me when I am dying!

Day of tears and late repentance,
Man ſhall rise to hear his sentence:
Him, the child of guilt and error,
Spare, Lord, in that hour of terror!

II.

 AY ſhall dawn that has no morrow,
Day of vengeance, day of sorrow,
As from Prophecy we borrow.

It ſhall burn, that day of trouble,
As a furnace heated double,
And the wicked ſhall be ſtubble.

O, what trembling, when the rifted
Skies ſhall ſhow the Judge uplifted,
And all ſtrictly ſhall be ſifted!

Trump ſhall sound a blaſt appalling,
On the grave's deep ſtillness falling,
Small and great before Him calling.

Death with fear ſhall be o'ertaken,
Nature to her base be ſhaken,
When the ſleeping dead ſhall waken.

Volume shall be brought, whose pages
Register the deeds of ages,
Whence the world shall have just wages.

When that Court shall hold its session,
Every mouth shall make confession,
Left unpunished no transgression.

How, alas! in that dread season,
Shall I answer for my treason,
When the righteous fear with reason?

Awful King, who nothing cravest,
Since Thyself full ransom gavest,
Save Thou me, who freely savest!

Me, for whom, with love so tender,
Thou didst leave Thy throne of splendor,
Jesus, do not then surrender!

Wearily for me Thou toiledst,
Diedst for me and Satan spoiledst:
Let not triumph whom Thou foiledst!

Thou, whose frown will be damnation,
Grant me earneſt of salvation,
Ere that day of conſummation!

Culprit-like, I, self-convicted,
Bluſhing, proſtrate, and afflicted,
Kneel for mercy unreſtricted.

Thou, who Mary's faith rewardedſt,
Pardon to the Thief accordedſt,
Me, too, trembling hope affordedſt.

Poor my prayers, but give ensample
Of Thy goodness rich and ample,
Leſt insulted Juſtice trample!

With Thy chosen flock unspotted,
Severed from the herd besotted,
Be my place that day allotted!

When Thy curse ſhall blaſt and wither,
Doom to hell and baniſh thither,
Bid me with the bleſſed, Come hither!

Care for me as one who feareth,
One who hafteth when he heareth,
When my solemn exit neareth!

When the light of that day flafhes,
And man rises from his afhes
At Thy bar account to render,
Spare then, Lord, the pale offender!

III.

AY of Vengeance and of Wages,
Fiery goal of all the ages,
Burden of prophetic pages !

Guilty wretches, vainly fleeing
From that flaming Eye, whose seeing
Searches all the depths of being.

Wakened by that Trump of Wonder,
Answering Earthquakes, roaring under,
Heave and split the ground asunder;

And the buried generations,
People of all times and nations,
Live again and take their ſtations,

Each immortal pale offender,
Round the Great White Throne of Splendor,
Striđ account to God to render;

Who, unmocked and unmistaken,
Shall pronounce the doom unshaken,
And long slumbering vengeance waken.

What if weighed and found deficient?
Standing at that bar omniscient,
Who hath righteousness sufficient?

Dreadful Majesty of Heaven!
Freely thy salvation's given,
Fount of Mercy, save me even!

Me, for whom Thou shame didst borrow,
Trod'st the paths of earthly sorrow,
Lose not on that dreadful morrow!

Seeking me Thou weary sankest,
All my cup of trembling drankest,
Nor from death, to save me, shrankest.

Must I sink yet to perdition?
God of Vengeance, grant remission,
Ere that Day of Inquisition!

Filled with fhame and confternation,
Lifting hands of supplication,
Spare me, God of my Salvation!

Let such grace be manifefted,
As on weeping Mary refted,
As was towards the Thief attefted!

Though no worth in me discerning,
Spurn not, though I merit spurning:
Rescue me from endless burning!

When divifion is effected
'Mong the race of men collected,
Leave me not with the rejected!

When Thy curse from Thee fhall sever,
Kindling hells, extinguifhed never,
Join me to Thyself forever!

From the afhes of contrition,
From the depths I make petition:
Grant my soul a safe dismiffion!

When that day ſhall snare th' unwary,
And ſhall guilty man unbury,
Spare me then, Dread Adversary!

IV.

AY of Prophecy ! it flashes,
Falling spheres together dashes,
And the world consumes to ashes.

O, what fear of wrath impending,
When the Judge is seen descending,
Inquifition ftrict intending !

God's awakening 'Trump fhall scatter
Summons through the world of matter,
And the Throne of Death fhall fhatter.

What amazement, when forgotten
Generations, dead and rotten,
Suddenly are rebegotten !

Book and Record universal
Shall be opened for rehearsal,
Whence the doom without reversal.

3

When by that dread Judge inspected,
Nothing ſhall pass undetected,
Unavenged nor uncorrected.

How ſhall I, a wretch unſtable,
Bide that hour inevitable,
When the juſt man scarce is able?

Dreadful King, from Thee, the Giver,
Flows salvation like a river:
Fount of Mercy, me deliver!

Thou, who, touched with my condition,
Cam'st to save me from perdition,
Be Thou mindful of Thy miſſion!

Let Thy death for my offences,
Horror of Thy soul and senses,
Be not void of consequences!

Blot my ſins, ere that reviſion,
Day of ultimate deciſion,
When Thy foes are in deriſion!

From my eyes repentance gushes,
O'er my cheeks spread crimson blushes:
Spare the worm Thy terror crushes!

Thou, who wert of old most gracious
Ev'n to sinners most audacious,
Is Thy mercy now less spacious?

Worthless all the prayers I offer:
Grace must seal what grace doth proffer,
Else I perish with the scoffer.

When Thou makest separation,
With Thy sheep assign my station,
Saints of every age and nation!

When the malison eternal
Banishes to fires infernal,
Bid me enter realms supernal!

Thou, who dost, with care unsleeping,
Keep that trusted to Thy keeping,
Save my eyes from endless weeping!

Day of tears, consuming, cruel,
With a burning world for fuel!
Man ſhall rise from glowing embers,
Made complete in all his members:
Ah! what plea will then be valid,
When the ſinner, trembling, pallid,
Waits to hear his sentence given?
Spare him then, O God of Heaven!

V.

AY of vengeance, end of scorning,
World in afhes, world in mourning,
Whereof Prophets utter warning!

O, what trembling, when the falling
Rocks and mountains hear men calling,
"Hide me from that face appalling!"

Freezing fear the blood will thicken,
Death and Hell be horror-ftricken,
When the myftic Trump fhall quicken

All the buried duft of ages,—
Monarchs, chieftains, ftatesmen, sages,
Actors on unnumbered ftages,—

Summoned to the dread recital
Of that Record ftrict and vital,
Basis of a juft requital.

Every mafk of falsehood riven, —
Guilt, from every covert driven,
Shall to punifhment be given.

'Mid the horror and confufion
Of that sorrowful conclufion
Of each miserable delufion,

Whither, ah! fhall I betake me?
Thou, O King, whose terrors fhake me,
Of Thy grace a trophy make me!

Jesus! by Thine incarnation,
By Thy miffion of salvation,
Then avert juft condemnation!

By Thy pity, love unfailing,
By the cross's bitter nailing,
Let not all be unavailing!

Dread Avenger of transgreffion,
Cleanse these lips that make confeffion,
Ere th' awards of that laft seffion.

Spare a culprit, groans faſt heaving,
Self-convicted, bluſhing, grieving,
In Thy power and grace believing.

Since Thy nature doth not vary,
Thou, who heard'ſt the Thief and Mary,
My transgreſſions blot and bury!

Worthless works behind me caſting—
Grace muſt save, not prayer nor faſting,
From the fire that's everlaſting.

On Thy right hand fix my ſtation
With the chosen generation,
In the ſheep-fold of salvation!

When Thy curse the wicked chases,
With the bleſt in heavenly places
Call me to Thy dear embraces!

Care for me, whom guilt abaſhes,
Proſtrate, contrite, heart as aſhes,
When that day of terror flaſhes!

Day of weeping and of wailing,
Human hearts and fates unveiling!
Then, when Time ſhall be no longer,
And the ſtrong yields to the Stronger,
Death and Hell their dead surrender,
And the Sea its own ſhall tender,
Multitudinous, unbounded
Generations rise aſtounded,
Each to answer for his ſinning,
He who lived at the beginning,
He who when the world is hoary,—
Spare, O, spare, Thou God of Glory!

VI.

AY of wrath and confternation,
Day of fiery consummation,
Prophefied in Revelation!

O, what horror on all faces,
When the coming Judge each traces,
Flaming, dreadful, in all places!

Trump fhall sound, and every fingle
Mortal slumberer's ears fhall tingle,
And the dead fhall rise and mingle:

All of every tribe and nation,
That have lived fince the creation,
Answering that dread citation.

Book, where actions are recorded,
All the ages have afforded,
Shall be brought and dooms awarded.

4

Judge, who fits at that affizes,
Shall, deceived by no disguises,
Try each work that man devises.

How fhall I, a wretch polluted,
Answer then to fins imputed,
When the juft man's case is mooted?

Awful Monarch of Creation!
Saving without compensation,
Save me, Fountain of Salvation!

Lose me not then, Jefus, seeing
I am Thine by gift of being,
Doubly Thine by price of freeing!

Thou, the Lord of Life and Glory,
Hung'ft a victim gafhed and gory:
Let not all be nugatory!

Pardon, Thou whose vengeance smiteth,
But whom mercy moft delighteth,
Ere that reck'ning day affrighteth!

As a culprit, ftand I groaning,
Blufhing, my demerit owning:
Sprinkle me with blood atoning!

Thou, who Mary's sins remittedft,
And the softened Thief acquittedft,
Likewise hope to me permittedft.

Weak these prayers Thy throne affailing;
But let grace, o'er guilt prevailing,
Save me from eternal wailing!

While the goats afar are driven,
'Mid Thy fheep me place be given,
Blood-wafhed favorites of Heaven!

While "Depart!" fhall doom and gather
Those to flame, address me rather:
"Come thou bleffed of my Father!"

In my final hour, when faileth
Heart and flefh, and my cheek paleth,
Grant that succor which availeth!

Day unutterably solemn!
Crypt and pyramid and column,
Ifle and continent and ocean,
Rocking with a fearful motion,
Shall give up, a countless number
Starting from their long, long flumber,
Horror ftamping every feature,
While is judged each finful creature,
End of pending controversy:
Spare Thou then, O God of Mercy!

VII.

AY of wrath, that day of days,
Present to my thought always,
When the world fhall burn and
blaze!

O, what trembling, O, what fear,
When th' Omniscient Judge draws near,
Scanning all with eyes severe!

When the 'Trump of God fhall sound
Through the vague and vaft profound
Of the regions under ground;

And th' innumerable dead,
Answering to that summons dread,
Shall forsake their dufty bed;

And that Book of ancient date
Shall be opened, whereon wait
Mighty iffues big with fate;

And each secret thing shall lie
Thenceforth bare to every eye,
Nought unpunished or passed by.

Ah, me! what shall I then plead,
Who for me then intercede,
When the just of help have need?

Thou, who dost, O Heavenly King,
Free forgiveness freely bring,
Let me drink of Mercy's Spring!

Thou didst empty and exhaust
Heaven for me: when such the cost,
Jesus, let me not be lost!

Wearily Thou soughtest me,
Bought'st me on th' accurséd tree:
Let it not all fruitless be!

Righteous Judge, who wilt repay,
Grant me pardon, ere that day
Of decision and dismay!

I, a finful man and base,
Blufhing, groaning o'er my case,
Seek and supplicate Thy grace.

Thou, who heardeft Mary's fighs,
Thou, who openedft Paradise
To the Thief, regard my cries!

Worthless are my prayers and **worse,**
But, good Lord, be not adverse,
Left I fink beneath the curse !

Set me, when at Thy command
All mankind divided ftand,
With the fheep at Thy right hand !

When th' insufferable doom
Shall the reprobate consume,
With Thy chosen give me room !

In the solemn hour of death,
When the earthly vanifheth,
O, receive my parting breath !

Ah! that day made up of tears,
When from aſhes reappears
Th' Adam of ſix thousand years,—

Who, by its red glare and gleam,
Sees, as in an awful dream,
Juſtice lift her trembling beam,—

Conscious on that hinge of fate
All things hang and heſitate :
Spare then, Lord, if not too late!

VIII.

 THAT dreadful day, my soul!
Which the ages fhall unroll,
When the knell of Time fhall
toll !

O, the terror and the fhame,
When the Judge with eyes of flame
Shall make piercing search of blame!

Suddenly the Trumpet's fhock
Doors of Hades fhall unlock,
And before Him all fhall flock.

Struck with wonder and dismay,
Death and Nature fhall obey
Summons to give up their prey.

Loudly each indictment dread
Shall in every ear be read
Of the living and the dead.

Every idle word and thought,
Every work in secret wrought,
Into Judgment ſhall be brought.

Scarce the juſt man's case is sure,
Scarce the heavens themselves are pure:
Ah! how then ſhall I endure?

Dreadful Potentate and high,
Who doſt freely juſtify,
Fount of Grace, my need supply!

Jeſus, mind the kind intent
Of Thy weary baniſhment,
And my ruin then prevent!

Let Thy paſſion and Thy pain,
All Thou ſufferedſt me to gain,
Be not barren and in vain!

Righteous Arbiter of fate!
Life and death upon Thee wait,
Pardon, ere it be too late!

Spare me, vileſt of the race,
Guilty, infamous and base,
Bluſhing mendicant of grace !

Though of ſinners I be chief,
Hear me, Thou who heard'ſt the Thief,
Driedſt the fount of Mary's grief!

All my prayers are guilty breath,
And the beſt nought meriteth :
But in mercy save from death!

When, disposed on either hand,
All mankind before Thee ſtand,
Set me with Thy chosen band!

When, O, terrible to tell !
Yawns inevitable Hell,
With the bleſſed bid me dwell!

When I reach the awful goal,
And Death's billows o'er me roll,
Care for my undying soul!

Day of weeping and surprise,
Opening tombs and opening eyes,
Rocking earth and burning ſkies !

Day of universal dread,
When the quick and quickened dead
Shall have solemn sentence said !

Then, O, then, when in despair,
Man ſhall speak or ſhriek the prayer,
" Spare me ! " God of Mercy, spare !

IX.

AY foretold, that day of ire,
Burden erſt of David's lyre,
When the world ſhall ſink in
fire !

O, what horror and amaze,
When at once on mortal gaze
All the Judge's pomp ſhall blaze!

When the Trumpet's myſtic blaſt,
To the world's four corners caſt,
Disentombs the buried Paſt ;

And from all the heaving sod,
From each foot of trampled clod,
Starts a multitude to God ;

And that Volume is unrolled
Wherein are minutely told
All men's doings from of old ;

While, from what is there contained,
Shall be judged a world arraigned,
And eternal fates ordained :

What defence can I then make,
To what Patron me betake,
When the righteous fear and quake?

King, who doſt all power poſſeſs,
Free Thy grace and limitless,
Save me, Fount of Bleſſedness!

Jeſus, Maſter, Thou doſt know
I Thy miſſion caused below,
All Thy weariness and woe!

Let Thy blood, that drenched the hilt
Of that sword unſheathed for guilt,
Be not vainly ſhed and spilt!

O my Judge, forgive, forget!
Cancel my tremendous debt,
Ere the sun of grace ſhall set!

Filled with shame I hang my head,
Blushes deep my face o'erspread :
Stay Thy lightnings fierce and red!

Thou canst darkest stains efface ;
Hast made monuments of grace
Of the vilest of the race.

My poor prayers please not repel !
Grace and goodness with Thee dwell :
Snatch me from the flames of Hell!

When Thou shalt discriminate,
Sheep from goats shalt separate,
Let me on Thy right hand wait !

When Thy sentence, smiting dumb,
Down to Hell shall banish some,
With the blessed bid me come!

To Thy care, O Kind as Just !
Heart all penitential dust,
I my end commit and trust !

Floods of tears that day fhall pour;
Man fhall wake to fleep no more;
Guilty, horribly afraid:
Spare him, Lord, whom Thou haft made!

X.

 O ! it comes, with ſtealthy feet,
Day, the ages ſhall complete,
When the world ſhall melt with
    heat !

O, what trembling ſhall there be,
When all eyes the Judge ſhall see,
Come to ſift iniquity !

Trump ſhall syllable command,
And the dead of sea and land
All before the Throne ſhall ſtand.

Death ſhall ſhudder, Nature too,
When the creature lives anew,
Called to render answer true.

Volume, that omitteth nought
Man e'er said or did or thought,
Shall for sentence then be brought.

6

When shall sit the Judge severe,
All that's dark shall be made clear,
Nothing unavenged appear.

What, alas! shall I then say,
To what Intercessor pray,
When the just shrink with dismay?

Awful King, since all is free,
Without merit, without fee,
Fount of Mercy, save Thou me!

Mind, O Jesus, Friend sincere,
How I caused Thy advent here,
Nor me lose who cost so dear!

Straying, I by Thee was sought,
On the cross with blood was bought:
Let it not be all for nought!

Righteous Judge! Avenging Lord!
Full remission me afford,
Ere that final day's award!

Groan I, like a culprit base,
Conscious guilt inflames my face:
Spare the suppliant, God of Grace!

Thou, who erſt didſt Mary clear,
And the dying Thief didſt hear,
Hope haſt given me to cheer.

Though my prayers create no claim,
Be propitious, Lord, the same,
Leſt I burn in endless flame!

Place among Thy ſheep provide,
From the goats me sunder wide,
Standing safe at Thy right ſide!

While " Depart!" to foes addreſſed
Baniſheth to woes ungueſſed,
Call me near Thee with the bleſſed!

Contrite pangs my bosom tear,
Heart as aſhes: hear my prayer,
Let my end be not despair!

On that day of grief and dread,
When man, rifing from the dead,
Shall eternal juftice face,
Spare the finner, God of Grace.

XI.

AY of wrath, that day of dole,
When a fire ſhall wrap the whole,
And the earth be burnt to coal!

O, what horror, smiting dumb
When the Judge of all ſhall come,
Sinful deeds to search and sum!

Trump's reverberating roar
Through the sepulchres ſhall pour,
Citing all the Throne before.

Death and Nature ſtand aghaſt,
While the dead in numbers vaſt
Rise to answer for the paſt.

Volume, writ by God's own pen,
Chronicling the deeds of men,
Shall be brought, and dooms be then.

When the Judge shall sit, behold!
What is secret He'll unfold,
No just punishment withhold.

Ah! what plea shall I prepare,
To what Patron make my prayer,
When the just well-nigh despair?

King, majestic beyond thought,
Whose free grace cannot be bought,
Save me, whose desert is nought!

O, remember, Jesus, I
Was the cause and reason why
Thou didst come on earth to die!

Me Thou sought'st with weary feet,
And my ransom didst complete:
Let such pity nought defeat!

Judge, inflexible and strict,
Pardon, ere that day convict
And th' unchanging doom inflict!

Like a criminal I sigh,
Blushing, penitently cry:
Pass, Lord, my offences by!

Thou, who Mary erst did'st bless,
Heard'st the Thief in his distress,
Hope hast given me no less.

Worthless are my prayers and vain,
But in love do not disdain,
Lest I reap eternal pain!

On Thy right hand grant me place
'Mid the sheep, a chosen race,—
Far from goats devoid of grace!

When the thunder of Thine ire
Headlong hurls to quenchless fire,
Let Thy welcome me inspire!

I entreat Thee, bending low,
Heart as ashes, full of woe,
Succor in my end bestow!

When upon that day of tears
Man from duſt again appears,
Fate depending on Thy nod:
Spare the ſinner then, O God!

XII.

 DAY of wrath! O day of fate!
Day foreordained and ultimate,
When all things here fhall termi-
nate!

What numbers horribly afraid,
When comes the Judge, in fear arrayed,
To try the creatures He hath made!

The blare of Trumpet, pealing clear,
Shall through the sepulchres career,
And wake the dead, and bring them near.

Aftonifhed Nature then fhall quail,
What time the yawning graves unveil,
And man comes forth, amazed and pale,

To answer: The o'erwritten scroll
Shall charge and certify the whole,
Whence fhall be judged each human soul.

7

The Judge enthroned ſhall bring to light
Whate'er is hid, in open ſight
Avenge and vindicate the right.

Ah! with what plea ſhall I then come,
When, terror-locked, each sense is numb,
And even righteous lips are dumb?

O King immortal and supreme,
Whose fear is great, whose grace extreme,
Make me to drink of Mercy's ſtream!

Remember, Jeſus, Thou didſt make
Thyself incarnate for my sake,
Leſt Hell inſatiate claim and take!

Thou soughteſt me when far aſtray,
Didſt on the cross my ransom pay:
Let not such love be thrown away!

Juſt Judge, of purity intense,
Remit my infinite offence,
Before that day of recompense!

Like one convinced of heinous deed,
I groan, I weep, I blush, I plead :
Lord, spare me in that hour of need !

Thou, who wert moved by Mary's tears,
Absolved the Robber from his fears,
Haſt given me hope in former years.

My prayers are worthless well I know ;
But, good, do Thou Thy goodness ſhow,
And save me from impending woe !

Number and place me 'mong Thy own,
Beneath the ſhelter of Thy Throne,
Until Thy wrath be overblown!

When that the almighty word ſhall leap
From out Thy Throne, Thy foes to sweep,
My soul in perfe&t safety keep !

In proſtrate worſhip, I implore,
With heart all penitent and sore :
Then care for me when life is o'er !

Ah! on that day of grief and dread,
And resurrection of the dead,
Of trial and of juſt award,
In wrath remember mercy, Lord!

<h1 style="text-align:center">XIII.</h1>

HAT day, that awful day, the laſt,
Reſult and ſum of all the Paſt,
Great neceſſary day of doom,
When wrecking fires ſhall all con-
sume !

What dreadful ſhrieks the air ſhall rend,
When all ſhall ſee the Judge deſcend,
And hear th' Archangel's echoing ſhout
From heavenly ſpaces ringing out !

The Trump of God with quickening breath
Shall pierce the ſilent realms of Death,
And ſound the ſummons in each ear :
" Arise ! thy Maker calls ! Appear ! "

From eaſt to weſt, from ſouth to north,
The earth ſhall travail and bring forth ;

As desert's sands and ocean's waves
Shall be the sum of empty graves.

Th' unchanging Record of the Past
Shall then be read from first to last ;
And out of things therein contained,
Shall all be judged and fates ordained.

No lying tongue, that truth diftorts,
Shall witness in that Court of Courts,
Each secret thing fhall be revealed,
And every righteous sentence sealed.

Ah! who can ftand when He appears ?
Confront the guilt of finful years ?
What hope for me, a wretch depraved,
When scarce the righteous man is saved ?

Dread Monarch of the Earth and Heaven!
For that salvation's great 'tis given ;
And fince the boon is wholly free,
O Fount of Pity, save Thou me !

Remember, Jefus, how my case
Once moved Thy pity and Thy grace,
And brought Thee down on earth to ftay:
O, lose me not, then, on that day!

I seek Thee, who didft seek me firft,
Weary and hungry and athirft;
Didft pay my ransom on the tree:
Let not such travail fruftrate be!

Juft Judge of vengeance in the end,
Now in the accepted time befriend!
My fins, O, gracioufly remit,
Ere Thou judicially fhalt fit!

Low at Thy feet I groaning lie;
With blufhing cheek, and weeping eye,
And ftammering lips, I urge the prayer:
O spare me, God of Mercy, spare!

When Mary Thy forgiveness sought,
Wept, but articulated nought,

Thou didſt forgive; didſt hear the brief
Petition of the dying Thief.

On grace thus great my hope is built
That Thou wilt cancel, too, my guilt;
That, though my prayers are worthless breath,
Thou wilt deliver me from death.

When Thy dividing rod of might
Appointeth ſtations oppoſite,
Among Thy ſheep grant me to ſtand,
Far from the goats, at Thy right hand!

And when despair ſhall seize each heart
That hears the dreadful sound, "Depart!"
Be mine, the heavenly lot of some,
To hear that word of welcome, "Come!"

I come to Thee with trembling truſt,
And lay my forehead in the duſt;
In my laſt hour do Thou befriend,
And glorify Thee in my end!

APPENDIX.—SEQUENCE.

A STATEMENT of the order observed in the celebration of Mass will beſt explain the nature and import of this term, in its application by the Romiſh Church to a large body of hymns,—Daniel, in the 5th volume of his learned and laborious work, "Thesaurus Hymnologicus," citing no less than eight hundred, the laſt one given being a new Sequence, composed in honor of the Virgin in 1855, "Sequentia de Beata Maria Virgine ſine Labe Concepta, Virgo Virginum Præclara."

The dispoſition of parts in the Mass is as follows, viz.: 1. THE INTROIT, which is the part sung or chanted when the prieſt *enters* within the rails of the altar. 2. THE COLLECT, or PRAYER. 3. READING OF THE EPISTLE, being, in the Mass for the Dead, 1 Cor. xv. 51–57, or Rev. xiv. 13. 4. THE GRADUAL, so called from its having been sung or chanted

8

formerly from the fteps (*gradus*) of the altar, clofing with the ALLELUIA. 5. THE TRACT, which is omitted when the Alleluia is sung; otherwise it is sung in the interval to prepare for the following. The primary meaning of the word (from *traho*, to protract or draw out) is adapted to suggeft either the use here indicated, i. e. to fill up time, or else to express the flow, mournful movement which characterizes the chant. 6. THE SEQUENCE, being, in the Mass for the Dead, the DIES IRÆ. 7. READING OF THE GOSPEL, being, in the Mass for the Dead, John v. 25–29. 8. THE OFFERTORY, which is a fhort sentence that varies. 9. THE SECRET, a brief prayer recited by the prieft in a very low tone of voice. 10. COMMUNION, or the application of the Mass. 11. POST-COMMUNION.

The Sequence, it will be seen, occupies a pofition exactly midway, being juft after the Gradual and Tract, and immediately before the Gospel. The Reading of the Gospel happening to be introduced by the words, " Sequentia Sancti Evangelii secundum ———," (The Continuation of the Holy Gospel according to ———,) some have supposed that the term Sequentia or Sequence was derived from this source. Michael Prætorius was of this opinion. But the

moft approved authorities give the following explanation of its origin.

From an early period, it was the cuftom of the
Latin Church to fing the Gradual with the Alleluia
between the Epiftle and the Gospel; the Gradual
being completed, the Alleluia followed; and in order
to give to the officiating prieft or deacon sufficient
time to prepare and ascend the ambon or pulpit, the
choir repeated and continued the laft syllable A
through a series of notes. This *neuma*, as it was
called, or mufical prolongation of a letter, was named
SEQUENTIA, because it was sequent to and governed
by the melody and rhythm of the Alleluia. At a
later period, this paflage of notes sung without text,
conftituting the original form of the Sequence, came
to have words set thereto, thereby preparing the
way for other changes; and forasmuch as the firft
effays of this kind were unmetrical in their ftructure,
the term *Prosa* or Prose was applied by way of dis-
tinction to this species of compofition; of which
Notker, surnamed the Stammerer, (Balbulus,) who
died in 912, canonized in 1514, is confidered to have
been the originator. Gradually, rhyme, so much
and so fondly cultivated in the Middle Ages, found
'ts way into these also; and from the twelfth century

onward, Sequences became proper metrical songs, differing from other hymns only in this, that the ftrophes, inftead of four, were made to consist of three or fix lines, according as they were double or fingle. To this rule, however, there were some exceptions. The name of Prose, although not ftrictly proper in its application to metrical compofitions, continued to be used, nevertheless, as a general title for all Sequences; and so we find the Dies Iræ bearing the appellation in the Mass-books of " Prosa Ecclefiaftica de Mortuis."

Defigned in the firft inftance, as alleged by Notker, merely to affift the memory in retaining the long-drawn, caudal melodies of the Alleluia, the defirableness of having other songs for the Mass than the Gloria in Excelfis, Kyrie, Credo, &c., songs eafier in ftru&ture, which could be joined in, not only by the choir, but also by the congregation,—perhaps, too, the wifh to introduce greater variety into the service, and bring the finging into closer relation with the objects of particular Church feftivals, which could be done more readily by these Sequences,—caused them to be multiplied greatly.

But the Roman ritual finally limited them to four, viz.: *Victimæ paschali laudis*, S. for Eafter Sunday;

Veni Sancte Spiritus, S. for Whitsunday and St. Peter's Day ; *Lauda Sion Salvatorem*, S. for Solemnity of Corpus Chrifti ; and *Dies Iræ*, S. Mass for the Dead and All-Souls' Day ; nevertheless, other Mass-books of diocefes and monaftic orders contain more Sequences. The Sequence firft named has a different metre from the other three, being one of those rare cafes in which the characteriftic triplet form of the ftrophe is departed from. The second named, Veni Sancte Spiritus, which Trench speaks of as " the lovelieft, though not the grandeft, of all the hymns in the whole circle of Latin sacred poetry," contains ten ftrophes of three lines each. Its author was Robert the Second, son of Hugh Capet, who ascended the throne of France in the year 997, and died in 1031. Like Henry the Sixth of England, of a meek and gentle dispofition, a lover of peace, he was ill suited to contend with the turbulent and reftless spirits who surrounded him, whose delight was in war. The next Sequence has twelve double ftrophes of fix lines each. It is commonly attributed to the so-called Angelical Doctor, St. Thomas Aquinas. The laft, which is the DIES IRÆ, grand and unapproachable in its excellence, comprises seventeen ftrophes of three lines each, and one of four lines.

ORIGIN OF LATIN RHYME.

WHILE it is true that the Latin hymns written during the firſt centuries of the Chriſtian era are, speaking generally, characterized by the absence of rhyme, and that the prevalence of rhyme belongs peculiarly and almoſt excluſively to the period intervening between the pontificate of Gregory the Great and that of Leo X., it would be a great error to suppose that rhyme was then firſt introduced, or that it was borrowed, as some have surmised, from the Romance or Gothic languages. If we look for its origin, we ſhall find preludings and anticipations of it in every one of the Latin poets, not excepting the oldeſt. Examples of both middle and final rhyme occur in all. In the Introduction to Trench's " Sacred Latin

Poetry," where this whole subject is ably discussed, we have a collation of many of these. Witness the following. An ancient author, quoted by Cicero, (Tusc. l. i. c. 28,) possibly Ennius, has this ·—

> Cœlum nitescere, arbores frondescere,
> Vites lætificæ pampinis pubescere,
> Rami baccarum ubertate incurvescere.

Of middle rhyme, we have in Ennius : —

> Non cauponantes bellum, sed belligerantes ;

In Virgil : —

> Limus ut hic durescit, et hæc ut cera liquescit ;

In Ovid : —

> Quem mare carpentem, substrictaque crura gerentem ;

Where also is found this example of leonine pentameter : —

> Quærebant flavos per nemus omne favos.

Of final rhyme, we have, in Virgil : —

> Nec non Tarquinium ejectum Porsenna jubebat
> Accipere, ingentique urbem obsidione premebat ;

Also : —

> Omnis campis diffugit arator,
> Omnis et agricola, et tutâ latet arce viator :

In Horace : —

> Non satis est pulcra esse poëmata ; dulcia santo,
> Et quocumque volent, animum auditoris agunto ;

Also . —

> Multa recedentes adimunt.   Ne fortè seniles
> Mandentur juveni partes, pueroque viriles.

Lucan abounds in examples.   Even the Latin prose-writers, it would seem, did not disdain now and then to play at rhyme, by putting rhyming words in juxtapofition.   Cicero has *florem et colorem* ; Pliny, *veram et meram* ; Plautus, *melle et felle* ; and so others.

Rhyme being thus shown to have been a thing known to the language from the earlieſt times, it may be thought surprifing, that what at a later period was so highly prized, and so fondly and so laboriously cultivated, should have been, during so many centuries, to such an extent, neglected ; having been apparently ſhunned rather than sought for, particularly by those great maſters of poetry who illuſtrated the Auguſtan age.   The fact is, that the ancient claſſic metres, though found occaſionally, as we have seen, toying with rhyme, never seriously

affected it ; and it was not until the fhackles imposed
by these had been wholly fhaken off, and a fimpler
and more natural verfification, based upon accent
inftead of quantity, had succeeded in eftablifhing its
juft claims over the Greek intruder, that the *régime*
of rhyme fairly commenced.

Gregorian Chant.

an - te thronum. 5. Li - ber scriptus pro-fe - re - tur, In quo totum
re-spon-su - ra. 6. Ju - dex er - go cum se-de-bit, Quidquid latet
il - lâ di - e! 11. Jus-te Ju - dex ul - ti - o - nis, Donum fac re -
not sit cassus! 12. In ge - mis-co tanquam re - us, Cul-pâ ru-bet
par-te dex-trâ! 17. O - ro sup-plex et ac-cli - nis, Cor contritum
be - ne - dic-tis!

con - ti - ne-tur, Un-de mundus ju - di - ce-tur.
ap-pa - re-bit, Nil in-ul-tum re-ma - ne-bit.
- mis-si - o - nis An-te di - em ra - ti - o - nis. 18. La-chry-mo-sa
vul-tus me-us: Suppli-can-ti par-ce, De-us!
qua-si ci - nis: Ge-re cu-ram me-l fi - nis!

di - es Il - la Qua re-sur-get ex fa-vil-lâ, Ju-di-can-dus

ho - mo re - us: Hu - ic er - go par - ce, De - us!

DIES IRÆ PARODIED.

WILLIAM HENRY NASSAU, Prince
of Orange — son of William II., Prince
of Orange, by the Princefs Mary, eldeft
daughter of Charles I. — was called to
the throne of England in 1689, in conjunction with
his wife, Mary, eldeft daughter of the deposed James
II., James having fled to France, and with his family
become penfioners of Louis XIV., who in 1692 made
a vigorous attempt to effect his reftoration. A treaty
formed in 1699, providing for the settlement of the
succeffion to the throne of the Spanifh empire on
the extinction of the eldeft branch of the house of
Auftria, was violated by Louis XIV. in accepting
the Spanifh throne for his grandson, the Duke of
Anjou, who thus became Philip V. of Spain. In
addition to this, on the death of James II. he gave a

further affront by acknowledging his son James king
of Great Britain and Ireland.

From the union of the French and Spaniſh crowns
in the Bourbon family, and the anticipated reſtoration of James II. and his son, the Pretender, to the
throne of England, a certain Catholic prieſt, it would
seem, thought himself warranted in predicting the
speedy downfall of Proteſtant Holland, the converſion of England, and the overthrow of Lutheranism
and Calvinism throughout Europe — not scrupling
with profane audacity to traveſty the celebrated Latin
Judgment Hymn, the Dies Iræ, in the ventilation
of his malignant vaticinations.   The following
“ Nenia Batavorum ” or Dutchman’s Ditty, is furniſhed by the great scholar Leibnitz, written, it is
said, in the year 1700.

The ſkill and dexterity ſhown by the parodiſt in
his manipulation of the original text are undeniable ;
but whatever may be thought of him as a poet, subsequent events have made it certain that he was no
prophet ; while the licentious irreverence amounting
to blasphemy, which leads him to put the “ Grand
Monarque ” in the place of Chriſt the Judge, is

quite ſhocking to all right feeling and good taſte.
Still, as one of the Curioſities of Literature, it pos-
ſeſſes much intereſt.   It is for this reason, and because it poſſeſſes a hiſtorical value, that we give it
here.

Dies iræ, dies illa,
Solvet fœdus* in favilla,
Teste Tago, Scaldi, Scylla.
     That day of wrath, how it ſhall burn
     And ſhall the league to aſhes turn,
     From Tagus, Scheldt, and Scylla learn.

Quantus tremor eſt futurus
Dum Phillippus eſt venturus
Has Paludes aggreſſurus !
     What trembling multitudes afraid,
     While Philip ſhall the land invade,
     And through the marſhes march and wade !

Tuba mirum spargens sonum
Per unita regionum
Coget omnes ante thronum.

    * The league between England and Holland.

The blare of trumpet making known
Through the united countries blown
Shall bring them all before the throne.

Mars ſtupebit et Bellona
Dum rex dicit : Redde bona
Poſt hoc vives sub corona.
    Mars and Bellona dumb ſhall ſtand
    What time the king ſhall give command :
    " Yield to my sceptre, self and land."

Miles scriptus adducetur,
Cum quo Gallus unietur
Unde leo subjugetur.
    His levied hoſts he forth ſhall call,
    And joined to these ſhall be the Gaul
    Therewith the lion to enthrall.

Hic Rex ergo cum sedebit,
Vera fides refulgebit,
Nil Calvino remanebit.
    Then when this King ſhall ſit and reign,
    Lo ! the true faith ſhall ſhine again,
    And nought to Calvin ſhall remain.

Quid sum miser tunc dicturus,
Quem patronum rogaturus,
Cum nec Anglus fit securus?
　　What fhall I say forlorn and poor,
　　What Patron sue then or procure,
　　When not the Englishman's secure?

Rex invictæ pietatis!
Depreffifti noftros * satis,
Si cadendum, cedo fatis.
　　King of unconquered piety!
　　Vexed haft thou ours sufficiently;
　　Falling, I yield to deftiny.

Pofthoc colam Romam, pie,
Effe nolo causa viæ,
Ne me perdas illa die.
　　Henceforth at Rome my vows I'll pay,
　　Will not be cause more of the way,
　　Left thou deftroy me on that day.

　　　　* Huguenots of France.

Pro Leone multa paſſus,
Ut hic ſtaret* eras laſſus
Tantus labor non ſit caſſus.
> Thou for the Lion much haſt borne,
> That he might ſtand haſt been much worn,
> Let not such toil of fruit be ſhorn !

Magne Rector liliorum,†
Amor, timor populorum,
Parce terris Batavorum.
> Great Ruler of the lilies, hear !
> The people's love, the people's fear,
> Spare thou the Dutchmen's lands and gear !

Ingemisco tanquam reus,
Culpa rubet vultus meus —
Cadam, niſi juvat Deus.
> Like one condemned, I make my plaint,
> Remembered faults my visage paint —
> Unleſs God aid, I 'll fall and faint.

* Formerly when France aided the Dutch.
† In alluſion to fleur-de-lis, or the lilies quartered in the royal arms of France.

Dum Iberim domuifti,
Lufitanum erexifti,
Mihi quoque spem dedifti.
    For that while thou haft conquered Spain,
    Haft Portugal upraised again,
    I too some hope may entertain.

Preces meæ non sunt dignæ,
Sed, Rex Magne, fac benigne,
Ne bomborum cremur igne.
    My worthlefs prayers no favor earn,
    But be, Great King, benign, not ftern,
    Left that by blazing bombs I burn !

Inter tuos locum præfta,
Ut Romana colam fefta,
Et ut tua canam gefta.
    Among thy own me reinftate,
    That I Rome's feafts may venerate,
    And thy achievements celebrate !

Confutatis calvi brutis,*

Patre,† nato, reſtitutis

Redde mihi spem salutis.

     When quelled the Bald-head's ſtupid horde,

     The father and the son reſtored,

     Then hope of safety me afford !

Oro supplex et acclinis

Calvinismus fiat cinis,

Lachrymarum ut ſit finis.

     Do thou, I humbly supplicate,

     All Calvinism extirpate,

     That so our tears may terminate.

* William, Prince of Orange, who was bald.

† James II. and his son, the Pretender

Stabat Mater

(DOLOROSA)

HYMN OF THE SORROWS OF MARY

TRANSLATED BY

ABRAHAM COLES, M. D., PH. D.

THIRD EDITION.

NEW YORK

D. APPLETON AND COMPANY

1891

PROEM.

HE celebrated Paffion Hymn, the Stabat Mater, is so conftantly affociated with the Dies Iræ that to mention the one is to suggeft the other. It has been thought, therefore, that a Tranflation of this Prosa likewise, made as literal as poffible, might be acceptable to some readers, and form a not unsuitable appendage to the former volume, by supplying a ready means of comparison between two productions, about which, down to this day even, there has been a difference of opinion as to which should be awarded the palm of superiority.

It is hardly neceffary to say that reference is here had to their lyrical merits only ; for while the devout Proteftant finds nothing in the Judgment Hymn to jar with his own religious convictions, he is necessarily offended in the Stabat Mater by a devotion he believes misdirected and idolatrous, in the adoration which it pays to the Virgin. He is aware, however, that in the formation of a critical estimate of the two, theological considerations have no right to enter; and certainly the most zealous Romanist will be constrained to admit that there has been no backwardness evinced on the part of those who are not of his faith to do ample justice to the lyric excellence of the latter. Some have gone so far as to place it above its great rival, but this is not the general judgment, nor is it ours.

Beautiful it undoubtedly is, and powerful in its pathos beyond almost anything that has ever been written; but it is nevertheless true (and the same indeed may be said of the Dies Iræ likewise) that it owes much of its power to make us admire and weep to the transcendent nature of its theme. Beyond controversy, the most affecting spectacle ever exhibited to the gaze of the universe, was that witnessed on Mount Calvary. That amazing scene — Jesus on the cross and his mother standing near — had been, of course, a familiar object of contemplation to all Christian hearts, centuries before the author wrote. His chief bufinefs therefore would be not to originate but reproduce.

Evidently the key-note of the Hymn is ftruck in the two firft lines, of which the language is wholly borrowed (bating the epithets, which are not in the manner of the sacred writers) from the Evangelift John, as found in the Latin verfion : *Stabat juxta crucem mater ejus.* This brief but wonderfully sug-geftive sentence, furnifhes an outline which the pooreft imagination would be capable of filling up in a degree. Every mother's heart, for example, would suffice to tell what an abyss of tears muft have gone to make up that hiatus in the narrative, which leaves solely to inference what were the feel-ings of her, who, without comprehending the mys-tery, ftood there gazing upward on the agonized face and writhing form of her divine Son, through the long hours of mortal anguifh during which he hung upon the cross.

But however spontaneous and natural, — however true, beautiful, and even poetic, — and however vivid the emotions of sorrow, terror, and pity, arifing out of these inftinctive and uninftructed perceptions,

there is a vagueness as well as vividness, and a re-
sulting incapacity to express clearly and adequately
what is so genuinely felt. The ability to do this is
rare, and rarer ftill the poetic faculty, whereby the
unwritten melody of the heart is accommodated to
all lips and sung in all ears. To say that the author
of the Stabat Mater poffeffed this power and achieved
this triumph is to beftow upon him and his work
the higheft praise.

Rude though he be, and a ftammerer of barbarous
Latin, he gives undeniable evidence of being a true
poet. He has clairvoyance and second fight. The
diftant and the paft are made to him a virtual here
and now. He is in Italy, but he is also in Judea.
He lives in the thirteenth century, but is an eye-
witness of the crucifixion in the beginning of the
firft. He has immediate vifion. All that is tran-
spiring on Golgotha is diftinctly pictured on the retina
of his mind's eye. And by the light which is in
him he photographs what he sees for the use of
others. His *ecce!* is no pointless indication, but an
actual fhowing. The wail he utters is a veritable
echo of that which goes up from the cross. Everything is true to nature and to life.

The Hymn confifts of two parts. The firft four verses give a description of the fituation and character of the actors in the drama, as pictorially powerful as scripturally juft. From this fruitful source have come all the Mater Dolorosas of the Painters. It is affumed, in accordance with the belief of the Fathers, that the prophecy of Simeon: "A sword fhall pass through thy own soul also," had then its proper fulfilment. In the remaining fix verses, the writer henceforth diffatisfied with the *rôle* of a spectator, seeks to identify himself with the tragic scene ; prays that he may be permitted to bear a part, not in the way of sympathy merely, but of suffering alfo, and this too, the same both in kind and degree ; that, enduring ftripe for ftripe, wound for wound, there might be to him in every ftage of the Redeemer's paffion, groan answering to groan.

It is now that the Franciscan appears quite as much as the Chriftian. Even when, as in the 8th verse, he quotes St. Paul (who speaks of " bearing about in the body the dying of the Lord Jesus "), he is evidently thinking of St. Francis. He would fain have repeated the miracle of the " Stigmata " in his

own person, — have an actual and visible reproduction of the print of the nails and the spear in his own
hands and feet and ſide. As " plagas " in the laſt
line of the same verse is used not unfrequently in the
sense, not so much of wounds as the marks and ap-
pearances left by wounds, it would correspond very
exactly with the ſtigmata named in the legend, and
moſt likely, in the author's use of it, it was intended
as a synonym. The poſſibility of such a literalness,
however incredible to us, would not be so to him.

This Hymn is full of the implied merit of suffering,
— its meritoriousness in itself. And this is probably
one of the reasons why it became such a favorite
with the Flagellants, otherwise called Brethren of
the Cross (Crucifrates) and Cross-Bearers (Cruciferi),
penitents who, in the thirteenth, fourteenth, and
fifteenth centuries went about in proceſſion day and
night, travelling everywhere, naked to the waist,
with heads covered with a white cap or hood, whence
they received likewise the appellation of Dealbatores,
ſinging penitential psalms, and whipping themselves
until the blood flowed. By their means it was that
the knowledge of this Hymn was firſt carried to
almoſt every country in Europe.

The authorſhip of the Stabat Mater, like that of the Dies Iræ, has been the ſubject of dispute. It has been variouſly ascribed — to Pope Innocent III., but backed by no evidence whatever; to one of the Gregories, (either the 9th, 10th, or 11th, which, is not ſtated,) on the authority of the old Florentine hiſtorian Antoninus, who lived in the fifteenth century; to John XXII., on the faith of the Genoese Chancellor and hiſtorian, Georgius Stella, who wrote a few years earlier than the laſt named, dying in 1420. The text, as supplied by him, the oldeſt perhaps extant, differs but little from that of the Miſſale Romanum, except that it contains three more verses. Others have referred its paternity, contrary to all probability, to St. Bernard. Dismiſſing all these as conjectures unsupported by proof, it is now generally conceded, that evidence both external and internal makes it wellnigh certain that the Hymn was the work of a Franciscan friar, a junior contemporary as well as brother of the author of Dies Iræ, named Jacobus de Benedictis, commonly called Jacopone, that is, the great Jacob. This latter name, it seems, was originally deſigned as a kind of nickname; the

syllabic suffix, *oné*, meaning in Italian great, having
been added by scoffing contemporaries by way of de-
rifion, on account of the ftrangeness of his appearance
and behavior. Indeed, if we may credit the ftories
told by Wadding, the Irifh hiftorian of the order,
himself one of the number, his conduct at times
so far exceeded the bounds of ordinary fanatical ex-
travagance, as to be totally irreconcilable with the
poffeffion of right reason. Wadding expreflly says
that he was subject to fits of insanity, leading him at
one time to enter the public market-place naked,
with a saddle on his back and a bridle in his mouth,
going on all fours ; and at another, after anointing
himself with oil, and rolling himself in feathers of
various colors, to make his appearance suddenly, in
this unseemly and hideous guise, in the midft of a
gay affembly gathered together at the house of his
brother on the occafion of his daughter's marriage, —
and this too, in disregard of previous precautionary
entreaties of friends, who, apprehenfive, it seems, at
the time they invited him that he might be guilty of
some crazy manifeftation or other, had begged him
not to do anything to difturb the wedding feftivities,
but to behave as an ordinary citizen.

The shocking circumstances under which he lost a pious and beloved wife (the fall of a scaffold upon which a large number of females were seated witnessing some spectacle), and the discovery after death that she wore a girdle of hair around her naked body as a means of mortification to the flesh, affected him, it is said, to such a degree, that he immediately resolved to abandon the world, and devote the remainder of his days to the severest penances. He accordingly gave up all his civil honors, and divided his estate among the poor. Uniting himself to one of the existing orders, he now went abroad as a monk, clothed in rags, and practising all manner of ascetic severities beyond what was required of him by the rules of his order.

It is charitable to suppose that the shock of his domestic calamity, while it awakened his religious sensibilities, had the effect at the same time of unsettling his reason, causing partial insanity. It is in no wise inconsistent with this supposition, that he was able to write poems of such excellence as the Stabat Mater, and that other one ascribed to him by Wadding: " Cur mundus militat sub vana gloria," &c.,

since it is well known that mental unsoundness on some one point is not neceſſarily incompatible with the normal exercise of the general powers of the mind. This medical fact was not so well underſtood in his time as now ; and when at the end of ten years he defired to be received by the Minorites, and they hefitated on account of his reputed insanity, their scruples were overcome by reading his work "On Contempt of the World," conceiving that it was impoſſible that an insane man could write so excellent a book. This would seem to have been a prose work, written probably in his own Italian vernacular, and therefore not to be confounded with the Hymn juſt referred to, which usually bears likewise the title of " De Contemptu Mundi."

As a Minorite he was not willing to become a prieſt, only a lay-brother. Very severe againſt him- self, he was, says Wadding, always full of defire to imitate Christ and suffer for Him. In an ecſtasy he imagined at times that he faw Him with his bodily eyes, and believed that Jesus often conversed with him, — calling him deareſt Jacob. Very frequently he was seen fighing ; sometimes weeping, sometimes

finging, sometimes embracing trees, and exclaiming,
" O sweet Jesus! O gracious Jesus! O beloved
Jesus !" Once when weeping loudly, on being afked
the cause, he answered : " Because Love is not
loved." This fine saying is not unworthy of the
author of the Stabat Mater.

For determining the genuineness of love he gives
these searching tefts. " I cannot know pofitively that
I love, yet I have some good marks of it. Among
others, it is a fign of love to God when I afk the
Lord for something and He does it not, and I love
Him notwithftanding more than before. If He does
contrary to that which I seek for in my prayer, and
I love him twofold more than before, it is a fign of
right love. Of love to my neighbor I have this fign :
namely, that when he injures me I love him not less
than before. Did I love him less, it would prove
that I had loved not him previoufly but myself." In
this acute appreciation of the figns and symptoms of
true love, he gives evidence certainly of no want of
fkill in spiritual diagnosis ; and were he equally sound
and discriminating in all parts of Chriftian doctrine
and experience as in this, it might have been quite

safe to truſt him with the cure of souls.   It may be
that his teſts are too severe and superhuman, and so
far erroneous.

On the subjugation of the senses he allegorizes
in this wise : " A very beautiful virgin had five brothers, and all were very poor.   And the virgin had a
precious jewel of great worth.   One brother was a
guitar-player, the second a painter, the third a cook,
the fourth a spice dealer, the fifth a pimp.   Each
was willing to use blandiſhments to get the ſtone.
The firſt was willing to play, and so on.   But ſhe
said : What ſhall I do when the muſic has ceased ?
In ſhort, ſhe remained firm, and gave the jewel to
none.   At length a great king came, who was willing
to raise her to be his bride, and give her eternal life
if ſhe would present him with the ſtone.   Where-
upon ſhe says : How can I, O my sovereign, to such
grace refuse the ſtone ; and so ſhe gave it him."   It
is plain that by the brothers are meant the Five
Senses ; by the virgin, the Soul ; and by the precious
jewel, the Will.

With his severe principles and severer ascetic life,
Jacopone could not fail to earneſtly denounce the

corruptions of his time in general, and especially the licentious manners, wickedness, and debaucheries of the priesthood, and the deeply sunken condition of the Church. Boniface III., who, prior to his elevation to the papal chair, had lived in friendly relations with Jacopone, having been deeply offended by some sharp censures directed against him, threw him into prison, — at the same time suspended over him the excommunication. Boniface one day passing the cell where Jacopone was, asked scornfully, "When will you come out?" He answered, "When you come in." Boniface's own imprisonment and unhappy end in 1303 set him at liberty.

It is related likewise how he baffled Satanic craft by superior craftiness of his own; but the details of these temptations are so childish and ridiculous that it would not be profitable to quote. Doubtless it is more fitting to weep than to laugh over the frenzies and follies of such a man, —

> " To see that noble and most sovereign reason
> Like sweet bells jangled out of tune and harsh."

His whole history gives a melancholy but instructive insight into the prevalent fanaticism and dark ness of the period. His death took place at an advanced age in 1306. "He died," says Wadding, "like the swan, finging, — having composed several Hymns juft before his death."

The number of Tranflations made of the Stabat Mater is scarcely exceeded by that of the Dies Iræ. Lisco, in his work devoted to this Prosa, gives or makes mention of eighty-three in all, complete and incomplete. With the exception of four done in Dutch, these are all German. A fimilar collection of Englifh verfions, although comparatively few in number, would not be without intereft. In attempting to add another to those already exifting, the present Tranflator has been moved by a defire to produce one more literal, if poffible, than any he has seen. He is not, he confeffes, friendly to free tranflations. Free, he has often observed, is another name for false. A counterfeit is put in the place of the genuine ; so that inftead of a Stabat we get only some worthless fubftitute. He honors that pains-taking religious scrupulofity which respects the sacredness of words as well as thoughts ; and fhuns all sacrilegious license and profane handling, — carry-

ing this reverence for the venerated text so far as
to be unwilling, if it can poffibly be helped, to vary
one jot or tittle, either in the way of fubftitution or
alteration.

He has no patience with that preposterous conceit,
sufficiently common, which imagines itself competent
to improve on great originals — whether for that matter these be in a foreign tongue or the vernacular,
and so applies to all tamperings with Englifh hymns
as well. It is much, he confiders, as if some absurd
novice of the brufh fhould undertake with a presumptuous hand to retouch a Raphael; or an irrev-
erent ftone-cutter, by the clumsy use of his chisel, to
improve a Venus de Medicis, or an Apollo Belvedere;
or some ignorant devotee to make some fine ftatue
of the Virgin finer by puerile adornments of dress,
trinkets, and glass beads. If the use of means
adapted to degrade a mafterpiece to the level of an
image be accounted a fin and an outrage, it is difficult to see why the impertinences of the cheap em-
bellifhments of every would-be tranflator of famous
originals, who aspires to be fine rather than faithful,
fhould not be regarded as equally criminal. It may

be, as Dryden says, "*almoſt* impoſſible to tranſlate
verbally and well;" but as the portrait of a friend is
worthless, however beautiful, unless it be a likeness,
so we hold a verſion muſt fail of its purpose and be
wanting in value, juſt so far as it is lacking in the
eſſential point of being a faithful representation, both
as to form and spirit, of that to which it relates.
What is here said, is meant, of course, to apply only
to what is deliberately put forth as a veritable translation ; and not to a production which avowedly uses
the text merely as a theme, profeſſing and claiming
to do no more.   In this case one may deviate as he
pleases.   It is excluſively his own buſiness.

With these views of the duties of a tranſlator, the
writer has aimed, however much he may have fallen
ſhort, to make his rendering a word for word reflection of the original, so far at leaſt as the rigorous
requirements of rhyme and rhythm would allow.
For the sake, too, of a closer rhythmic conformity,
he has sought even to preserve the muſical quad-
ruplications of the female rhymes found in the second
and ſixth verses.   The text adopted is that of the
Roman Miſſal, except in one or two inſtances where
another reading has been preferred.

To make the resemblance between the two Hymns ſtill more complete, the Stabat Mater, like the Dies Iræ, has been moſt fortunate in its muſical alliances ; having been made the theme of some of the moſt celebrated compoſitions of the moſt eminent composers. It was set to muſic in the ſixteenth century by the famous papal chapel maſter, Paleſtrina ; and his compoſition is ſtill annually performed in the Siſtine Chapel during Holy Week. It is sung like-wise in connection with the feſtival of the Seven Sorrows of the Virgin. The compoſition of Pergoleſi, the laſt and moſt celebrated of his works, made juſt before his death and left unfiniſhed, has never, down to the present day, been surpaſſed, if equalled, in the eſtimation of critics. It is set for two voices, with accompaniments.

Tieck, in his Phantasus, Vol. 2d, p. 438, (edition of 1812,) thus speaks of the compoſition of Pergoleſi and the Hymn itself: " The loveliness of sorrow in the depth of pain, the smiling in tears, the childlike-ness, which touches on the higheſt heaven, had to me never before risen so bright in the soul. I had to turn away to conceal my tears, especially at the place : 'Videt suum dulcem natum.' How significant, that the Amen, after all is concluded, still sounds and plays in itself, and in tender emotion can find no end, as if it were afraid to dry up the tears, and would still fill itself with sobbings. The poetry itself is touching and profoundly penetrating; surely the poet sang those rhymes : 'Quæ mœrebat, et dolebat cum videbat,' with a moved mind." It is a tradition, that the great impression which the Stabat Mater of the young artist (Pergolesi) made on its first performance, inflamed another musician with such furious envy, that he struck down the young man as he was coming out of the church. This tradition has long ago been disproved, but as Pergolesi died early, it may, as one remarks, be permitted to the poet to refer to this story, and allow him to fall as a victim of his art and inspiration. He was born 1704—11 at Jesi, and died 1737 at Torre del Greco, at the foot of Mount Vesuvius, where he had retired on account of his weakened health. The recent composition of Rossini is popular and pleasing, but more operatic than ecclesiastical, and so is better suited to the concert-room than the church.

The names of other diftinguished composers might be cited, such as Aftorga, Haydn, Bellini, and Neukomm. Aftorga's principal work was his Stabat Mater, the MS. of which is ftill preserved at Oxford, he having lived a year or two in England. He was a native of Sicily, and died in 1755. Haydn's was published in the year 1781.

We give below a condensed view of the various readings taken from Lisco; and as the Hymn is usually divided into three-line Strophes, making in all twenty, the references will be to these : —

Strophe 1,	line	3.	Dum — Quâ.
2,	"	2.	Contriftatam — Contriftantem.
4,	"	2.	Et tremebat — Pia mater — Dum videbat et tremebat.
5,	"	2.	Chrifti matrem fi — Matrem Chrifti cum.
5,	"	3.	In tanto — tanto in.
6,	"	1.	Quis non poffit — Quis non poteft — Quis poffit non.
8,	"	1.	Videns — Vidit.
8,	"	2.	Morientem — Moriendo.
8,	"	3.	Dum emifit — amifit.
9,	"	1.	Pia mater — Eja mater.
10,	"	3.	Ut fibi — Et fibi ; ut tibi ; ut ipfi ; fibi ut.
11,	"	3.	Valide — vivide.
12,	"	2.	Jam dignati — Tam dignati.

Strophe 12, line 3.   Pœnas pro me — Pœnas mecum.
        13,   "   1.   Fac me vere tecum — Fac me tecum pie.
        14,   "   2.   Te libenter — Et me tibi — Tibi me con-
                            sociare.
        14,   "   3.   In planctu — Cum planctu.
        15,   "   2.   Mihi jam — Mihi tam.
        16,   "   2.   Suæ sortem — Fac consortem.
        16,   "   3.   Plagas recolere — Plagis te colere.
        17,   "   2.   Cruce hac — Cruce fac me hac beari —
                            Cruce fac.
        17,   "   3.   Ob amorem — Et cruore.
        18,   "   1.   Inflammatus et accensus — Flammis urar
                            ne (ne urar) succensus.
        20,   "   3.   Gloria — Gratia.

The Stabat Mater of Haydn has this for the
eighteenth Strophe : —

> Flammis orci ne succendar
> Per te, virgo, fac, defendar,
> In die judicii.

The Carmelite Miſſal gives for the nineteenth
Strophe the following : —

> Chriſte, cum ſit hinc exire
> Da per matrem me venire
> Ad palmam victoriæ.

The change made in some copies of the seventeenth Strophe, of the original " Cruce hac inebriari," into " Cruce fac me hac beari," is fignificant of some exception having been taken to the great ftrength, not to say the audacity, of the author's metaphor, — the drunkenness of love.

SEQUENTIA DE SEPTEM DOLORIBUS BEATÆ VIRGINIS.

I.

STABAT Mater dolorosa
Juxta crucem lachrymosa
    Quâ pendebat Filius ;
Cujus animam gementem,
Contristantem et dolentem,
    Pertransivit gladius.

II.

O quam tristis et afflicta
Fuit illa benedicta
    Mater Unigeniti !
Quæ mœrebat et dolebat
Et tremebat, cum videbat
    Nati pœnas Inclyti.

HYMN OF THE SORROWS OF MARY.

I.

STOOD th' afflicted Mother weeping,
Near the crofs her ftation keeping,
   Whereon hung her Son and Lord;
Through whose spirit sympathizing,
Sorrowing and agonizing,
   Also paffed the cruel sword.

II.

O how mournful and diftreffèd
Was that favored and moft bleffèd
   Mother of the Only Son!
Trembling, grieving, bosom heaving,
While perceiving, scarce believing,
   Pains of that Illuftrious One.

III.

Quis eſt homo, qui non fleret,
Matrem Chriſti ſi videret
   In tanto supplicio?
Quis non poſſet contriſtari
Piam matrem contemplari
   Dolentem cum Filio?

IV.

Pro peccatis suæ gentis
Vidit Jesum in tormentis
   Et flagellis subditum ;
Vidit suum dulcem natum
Morientem, desolatum,
   Dum emiſit spiritum.

V.

Pia Mater, fons amoris !
Me sentire vim doloris
   Fac, ut tecum lugeam.
Fac, ut ardeat cor meum
In amando Chriſtum Deum
   Ut Sibi complaceam.

III.

Who the man, who, called a brother,
Would not weep, saw he Chrift's mother
    In such deep diftrefs and wild?
Who could not sad tribute render
Witneffing that mother tender
    Agonizing with her Child?

IV.

For His people's fins atoning
Him fhe saw in torments groaning,
    Given to the scourger's rod ;
Saw her darling Offspring, dying
Desolate, forsaken, crying,
    Yield His spirit up to God.

V.

Make me feel thy sorrow's power,
That with thee I tears may fhower,
    Tender Mother, fount of love !
Make my heart with love unceafing
Burn towards Chrift the Lord, that pleafing
    I may be to Him above.

VI.

Sancta Mater, istud agas,
Crucifixi fige plagas
     Cordi meo valide.
Tui nati vulnerati,
Tam dignati pro me pati
     Pœnas mecum divide.

VII.

Fac me tecum vere flere,
Crucifixo condolere,
     Donec ego vixero.
Juxta crucem tecum stare,
Te libenter sociare,
     In planctu desidero.

VIII.

Virgo virginum præclara,
Mihi tam non sis amara,
     Fac me tecum plangere;
Fac ut portem Christi mortem,
Passionis fac consortem,
     Et plagas recolere.

VI.

Holy Mother, this be granted,
That the Slain One's wounds be planted
    Firmly in my heart to bide.
Of Him wounded, all aftounded, —
Depths unbounded for me sounded, —
    All the pangs with me divide.

VII.

Make me weep with thee in union;
With the Crucified, communion
    In His grief and suffering give:
Near the crofs with tears unfailing
I would join thee in thy wailing
    Here as long as I fhall live.

VIII.

Maid of maidens, all excelling,
Be not bitter, me repelling,
    Make thou me a mourner too;
Make me bear about Chrift's dying,
Share His paffion, fhame defying,
    All His wounds in me renew:

IX.

Fac me plagis vulnerari,
Cruce hac inebriari
   Ob amorem Filii.
Inflammatus et accensus,
Per te, Virgo, fim defensus
   In die Judicii.

X.

Fac me cruce cuftodiri,
Morte Chrifti præmuniri,
   Confoveri gratia.
Quando corpus morietur,
Fac ut animæ donetur
   Paradifi gloria.

IX.

Wound for wound be there created;
With the Crofs intoxicated
 For thy Son's dear sake, I pray —
May I, fired with pure affection,
Virgin, have through thee protection
 In the solemn Judgment Day.

X.

Let me by the Crofs be warded,
By the death of Chrift be guarded,
 Nourifhed by divine supplies.
When the body death hath riven,
Grant that to the soul be given
 Glories bright of Paradise.

REMARKS.

NO admiration of the lyric excellence of the Stabat Mater fhould be allowed to blind the reader to those objectionable features which muft always suffice, as they have hitherto done, to exclude it from every hymnarium of Proteftant Chriftendom. For not only is Mary made the object of religious worfhip, but the incommunicable attributes of the Deity are freely ascribed to her. Her agency is invoked as if fhe were the third person of the Trinity, or had powers coördinate and equal.

Plainly it is the province of the Holy Ghoft, and not of any creature, to "work in us to will and to do;" to effect spiritual changes; to "take of the things of Chrift and fhow them unto us,"—and yet these are the very things which fhe herself is afked to accomplifh for the suppliant. "Fac," alone, afide

from potential equivalents, is used at leaft nine times,
— a form of expreffion manifeftly inappropriate un-
lefs addreffed to one capable of acts causal and original and therefore divine. Not content, it seems,
with making her a fountain of supernatural influence,
a succedaneum of the Holy Ghoft, her efficiency
is extended to the performance likewise of the work
affigned to the Son, —

> Per te, Virgo, fim defensus
> In die Judicii, —

an expreffion of reliance on her rather than on Him
to ward off in that day the demands of divine juftice.
Mariolatry here culminates. It could not well be
carried farther.

Confidering that the pofition here given to the
mother of Chrift receives not a particle of counte-
nance anywhere in the New Teftament, one is led
to wonder how those who accepted its teachings
could ever have fallen into so awful an error. If
prayer of any kind addreffed to her were laudable or
lawful, how can it be explained that all the sacred
writers are so intensely reticent upon the point that
it is not poffible to find written so much as a fingle

syllable to authorize it, or a solitary example to sanction it ?   It is remarkable that Chrift, while here on
earth, did not hefitate to rebuke His mother on a
certain occafion when fhe manifefted a dispofition to
intrude her maternal human relation into the sphere
of His divinity, saying : " Woman, what have I to do
with thee ? "   At another time, upon being told that
His mother and His brethren ftood waiting without,
He said, " Who is my mother ? and who are my
brethren ? " and ftretching forth His hand toward
His disciples, He said, " Behold, my mother and my
brethren ?   For whosoever fhall do the will of my
Father which is in heaven, the same is my brother
and fifter and mother."

Everybody muft feel that there is a sublime propri-
ety in this declarative poftponement, once for all, of
flefhly relationfhips to the spiritual ; and that it would
be infinitely unbecoming in Him, who is the Creator
of all and the Judge of all, to be a respecter of persons, swayed as men are swayed by the fond par-
tialities of blood and kindred.   Upon this principle
it is easy to account for the flight mention made of
Chrift's mother in the Evangelifts, and the entire

absence of any allufion to her in the reft of the New Teftament. Even the Apoftle John, to whose loving care fhe was committed, and who took her to his own house, neither in his Epiftles nor in the Apocalypse names her so much as once. Paul, the moft voluminous of the New Teftament writers, is wholly filent in regard to her.

When the people of Lyftra were making ready to pay divine honors to Barnabas and Paul, they, hearing of it, " rent their clothes, and ran among the people, crying out and saying, Sirs, why do ye these things ? " If these revolted at the idea of being made the objects of religious worfhip, can we suppose that supreme form of it lefs fhocking to the soul of Mary, which is neceffarily implied in addreffing her as the omniscient and omnipresent hearer and answerer of prayer ? Such honor is difhonor. It is an offering of robbery. It robs God.

STABAT MATER.

(SUNG ON EVERY FRIDAY DURING LENT.)

NO. 1.   *As sung in the Churches at Rome.*

GREGORIAN CHANT.
From the " Catholic Psalmist."

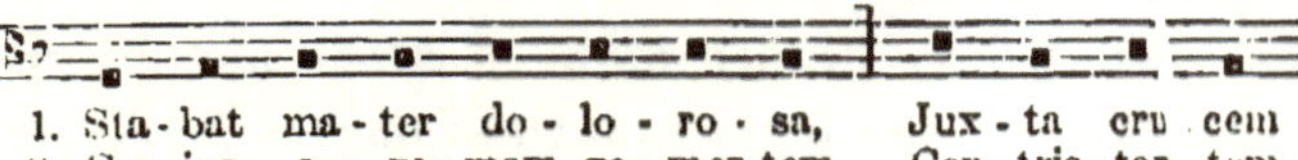

3. O quam tristis et afflicta
Fuit illa benedicta
Mater Unigeniti !

4. Quæ mœrebat et dolebat
Et tremebat cum videbat
Nati pœnas inclyti.

5. Quis est homo, qui non fleret,
Matrem Christi si videret
In tanto supplicio?

6. Quis non posset contristari,
Piam matrem contemplari
Dolentem cum filio.

7. Pro peccatis suæ gentis
Vidit Jesum in tormentis
Et flagellis subditum.

8. Vidit suum dulcem natum
Morientem, desolatum
Dum emisit spiritum.

9. Pia mater, fons amoris !
Me sentire vim doloris
Fac, ut tecum lugeam.

10. Fac, ut ardeat cor meum
In amando Christum Deum,
Ut Sibi complaceam.

11. Sancta mater, istud agas
Crucifixi fige plagas
Cordi meo valide.

12. Tui nati vulnerati
Tam dignati pro me pati
Pœnas mecum divide.

13. Fac me tecum pie flere
Crucifixo condolere
Donec ego vixero.

14. Juxta crucem tecum stare
Et me tibi sociare
In planctu desidero.

15. Virgo virginum præclara
Mihi tam non sis amara,
Fac me tecum plangere.

16. Fac ut portem Christi mortem
Passionis fac consortem
Et plagas recolere.

17. Fac me plagis vulnerari
Cruce hac inebriari
Ob amorem filii.

18. Inflammatus et accensus
Per te, virgo, sim defensus
In die judicii.

19. Fac me cruce custodiri
Morte Christi præmuniri
Confoveri gratia.

20. Quando corpus morietur
Fac ut animæ donetur
Paradisi gloria.

STABAT MATER.—Chant for Four Voices.

MADONNA DI SAN SISTO

Stabat Mater

(SPECIOSA)

HYMN OF THE JOYS OF MARY

TRANSLATED BY

ABRAHAM COLES, M. D., Ph. D.

SECOND EDITION.

NEW YORK

D APPLETON AND COMPANY

1891

STABAT MATER

(SPECIOSA).

R. PHILIP SCHAFF — whose voluminous contributions to the literature and hiftory of the Chriftian Church reflect the higheft honor upon American scholarfhip — in a recent number of " Hours at Home " (May, 1867), has, thanks to an eye that nothing escapes, been at the trouble of reproducing, with learned and inftructive comments for the benefit of readers on this fide of the Atlantic, a newly discovered STABAT MATER, being a Nativity Hymn, written it is supposed by the same hand as the Paffion Hymn, so that hereafter, as he remarks, there will be two Stabats — the *Stabat Mater Dolorosa*, and the *Stabat Mater Speciosa* ; the one setting forth the Joys, the other the Sorrows, of the Virgin Mother at the Manger and the Crofs.

The revival of this long-loft Hymn in our time, after five centuries of forgetfulnefs, is due to A. F. Ozanam, who, in a work on the Franciscan Poets ("Les Poëtes Franciscains en Italie au XIIIe siècle, avec un Choix de petites Fleurs de Saint François, trad. de l'Italien," Paris, 1852), has given it once more to the world. Hitherto there have been but two tranflations of the Hymn — one into German, by Cardinal Diepenbrock; the other, into Englifh, by Neale, made juft before his death. This Dr. Schaff copies in the article referred to. Both Ozanam and Neale affume an identity of authorfhip for the two: and Neale infers, from the want of finifh and the imperfect rhymes, that the *Mater Speciosa* was compofed firft; but we entirely agree with Dr. Schaff in thinking that internal evidence, alone, makes it certain that this is not the case. Ingenious and exact as is the parallel, it is easy enough to see which was firft and which was second. If twins, the *Mater Dolorosa* muft have been the elder. It is impoffible that " Pertranfivit jubilus " was written before " Pertranfivit gladius."

But we doubt, we confefs, a fimultaneous birth,

or even a common parentage. In the absence of
hiftorical proof, we fhould think it far more probable, that the *Mater Speciosa* was the work of some
admiring imitator, after the other had become famous ;
who, not fully satisfied with his performance, was
waiting to give it its final touches when he fhould have
decided between this and that; which explains the
supernumerary lines appended to the eighth ftrophe.*
Affuming the priority of the *Mater Dolorosa*, about
which there cannot be a particle of doubt, it is difficult to conceive that the other could have been the
work of the same pen. It is only the celebrity of
an original which invites parody. A man would
hardly be a model to himself. True merit, if not
unconscious, is usually modeft, and it is not likely
that our author, at the time he wrote, placed any
special value upon his produ&ion ; much lefs fore-
saw its after succefs. Why then fhould he, in preparing a hymn on the Nativity, prepofteroufly seek
to tie himself down to the use of the self-same

* " Hunc ardorem fac communem
Ne me facias immunem
Ab hoc defiderio."

words and order of words which he had happened
to employ in compofing a hymn on the Crucifixion?
After this had grown into public favor, it is easy to
underſtand, how some one else, other than the author, ſhould be prompted to attempt so curious and
difficult a taſk, because the verbal semblance would
aid, by aſſociation, in exciting ſimilar emotions of
reverent intereſt and sympathiſing tendernefs.   It is
right to ſtate, however, that opposed to this conclu-
ſion is the hiſtorical teſtimony of a second edition of
the Italian Poems of Jacopone (Laude di Frate Jacopone da Todi), publiſhed at Brescia, in 1495, which
contains, in an appendix, several Latin poems ascribed to him ; among which, according to Brunet,
are found both this *Mater Speciosa*, and the *Mater
Dolorosa*, as well as the *De Contemptu Mundi*. There
may be other evidence in support of this opinion, of
which we are ignorant ; but as the case ſtands, we
are compelled to adhere to the belief of a twofold
authorſhip ; and accept the above only as supplying
proof of the earlineſs of its origin.

'That the new found Stabat is not wanting in those
qualities which have attracted to its illuſtrious pro-

totype the admiring regards of men through so
many generations, teftifies to the fkill of the writer.
The ftructural correspondence between the two is
kept up throughout. Grief and gladnefs are seen
to go hand in hand, finging as they go, to the same
sweet time and measure. Were it only poetry and
not prayer — mere apoftrophe and not religious homage — we would be content ; but, alas ! there clings
to one and the other the fatal taint of idolatry ; and
we are not permitted to wink out of fight so un-
speakable an offense againft the purity of the unfhared
worfhip of the infinite Jehovah.

Happily we have other hymns on the Nativity,
againft which this objection does not lie. Milton's,
for example, the grandeft of them all, is wholly to
" the Infant God," not the human mother. It
divides not its worfhip. It fings and celebrates but
the One, and " prevents " the dawn and " the ftar-
led wizards," that it may be firft with its exclufive
offering " to lay it lowly at His blefled feet." Two
fimple and sweet lines at the close comprise all that
is said of the virgin mother :

> " But see, the virgin bleft
> Hath laid her Babe to reft."

They ſtand prefixed to the Cradle Hymn of Mrs. Browning, and may have ſuggeſted that divine lullaby, " The Virgin Mother to the Child Jesus." It is too long to give entire, but a ricochet extract may ſuffice to exhibit its general scope, and furniſh material for an intereſting and inſtructive comparison with its mediæval rival :

" Sleep, ſleep, my Holy One !
My fleſh, my Lord ! — what name ?   I do not know
A name that seemeth not too high or low,
Too far from me or heaven.
My Jesus, *that* is beſt ! that word being given
By the majeſtic angel whose command
Was softly as a man's beseeching aid,
When I and all the earth appeared to ſtand
In the great overflow
Of light celeſtial from his wings and head —
Sleep, ſleep, my Saving One !
And art Thou come for saving, baby-browed
And speechleſs Being — art Thou come for saving ?

.   .   .   .

Art come for saving, O my weary One ?
Perchance this ſleep, that ſhutteth out the dreary
Earth-sounds and motions, opens on Thy soul
High dreams on fire with God.

.   .   .   .

Suffer this mother's kifs,
Beſt thing that earthly is.

. . . .

Thus noiselefs, thus.   Sleep, ſleep my dreaming One !

. . . .

I 'm 'ware of you, heavenly Presences !

. . . .

Unsunned i' the sunſhine !   I am 'ware.   Ye throw
No ſhade againſt the wall !

. . . .

I fall not on my sad clay face before ye —
I look on His.

. . . .

Ye are but fellow-worſhippers with me !
Sleep, ſleep, my worſhipped One !
We sate among the ſtalls of Bethlehem.
The dumb kine from their fodder turning them,
Softened their horny faces.

. . . .

The ſimple ſhepherds from their ſtar-lit brooks,
Brought viſionary looks,
As yet in their aſtonied hearing rung
The ſtrange sweet angel-tongue.
The magi of the Eaſt, in sandals worn
Knelt reverent.

. . . .

So let all earthlies and celcftials wait
    Upon Thy royal ftate.
    Sleep, fleep my kingly One !

   .   .   .   .

    I am not proud — *not proud !*
Albeit in my flefh God sent His Son,
Albeit over Him my head is bowed
As others bow before Him, ftill my heart
Bows lower than their knees.   O centuries,

   .   .   .   .

Whose murmurs seem to reach me while I keep
    Watch o'er this fleep —
Say of me as the Heavenly said, ' Thou art
The bleffedeft of women ! ' — *bleffedeft,*
Not holieft, not nobleft — no high name
Whose height misplaced may pierce me like a fhame,
When I fit meek in heaven.   For me, for me
God knows that I am feeble like the reft."

   .   .   .   .

We fhould know that a woman wrote this.   It is
a woman's utterance, and the truer because it is so.
Great is the myftery of maternity ; great is the joy
of a mother over her firft-born.   But, in the experience of the mother of our Lord, it was more
than the common myftery and the common joy.

Heaven had come down to her. She, a lowly maiden, of meek thoughts, living in retirement, had, not long before, been surprised by an angelic embassage, authenticating her as the chosen inftrument of a ftupendous manifeftation, even the revelation of the great myftery of Godlinefs, God manifeft in the flefh, and that flefh her flefh — a holy link born of her miraculous motherhood. She had felt the awe of a wondrous o'erfhadowing, and the thrill of a divine quickening, and the joy of a growing burden, and had sung her exultant *Magnificat*, and had been full of wonderings and worfhippings, long before the crowning beatitude of the bringing forth, and the seeing, and the hearing, and the laying in the bosom, and the chanting of the *Glcria in Excelsis* of the angels, and the homage of the fhepherds, and the proftrations of the magi. Was fhe therefore proud? Proud! Was fhe not therefore humble, yea, humbler than the humbleft? Who ought to kneel so low as fhe? O for a humility as deep as the grace is high! No room here for the petty elations of vanity. To conceive of her as fitting queen of heaven, arrogating higheft titles, and receiving, well-

pleased, the kneeling homage of men and of angels,
— what an indecency! How it vulgarizes and de-
grades her; such an inverſion of nobleneſs; such
an emptying of her true honor and proper glory,
which conſiſt in a peerleſs meekneſs, bowing ever
lower and lower at the footſtool, and her heart bowing ſtill lower than her knees! Call me " Bleſſed,"
but call me

> " no high name
> Whose height misplaced may pierce me like a ſhame
> When I ſit meek in heaven."

There is one other hymn on the same theme by
Craſhaw, so full of paſtoral sweetneſs, that we cannot forbear transcribing it here. Craſhaw, it is said,
formed his ſtyle on the moſt quaint and conceited
school of Italian poetry — that of Marino; and
there is often, it muſt be admitted, a ſtrained ex-
preſſion in his verses; but there are also many exquiſite touches of beauty and tenderneſs, and a
ſtrength withal which more than compensates for
an occaſional harſhneſs. Of all his writings, he is
beſt known, perhaps, by his verſion of the Dies
Iræ. In 1634 he publiſhed a volume of Latin

poems under the title of *Epigrammata Sacra*, in
which occurs that celebrated verse on the miracle at
Cana : —

    " Lympha pudica Deum videt et erubuit."

    " The modeſt water saw its God and bluſhed."

It is a curious faƈt that both Milton and Dryden
have each been credited with the authorſhip of the
line as given in Engliſh, varied only by the subſtitu-
tion of the epithet " conscious " for " modeſt."

His " Hymn on the Nativity as sung by Shep-
herds," given below, was probably suggeſted by
Correggio's far-famed piƈture in the Dresden Gal-
lery, called " La Notte " (The Night), and forms
a fit companion to it. Piƈture and poem have common attributes, so that it may properly be said,
that the one is the other, — that the poem is a
piƈture, and the piƈture a poem. In both, the form
of the Divine Infant is finely imagined as the radi-
ant centre of a supernatural illumination dazzling to
all eyes in the picture except those of the virgin
mother, while ſigns of daybreak are seen along the
eaſtern horizon, emblem of " the dayspring from on
high : " —

" Gloomy night embraced the place
Where the noble Infant lay :
The Babe looked up and showed its face —
In spite of darkness it was day.
We saw Thee in Thy balmy neft,
Bright dawn of an eternal day —
We saw Thine eyes break from the Eaft,
And chase their trembling fhades away,
We saw Thee and we blefs'd the fight —
We saw Thee by Thine own sweet light.

She fings Thy tears afleep, and dips
Her kiffes in Thy weeping eyes ;
She spreads the red leaves of Thy lips,
That in their buds yet blufhing lie ;
Yet when young April's hufband-fhowers
Shall blefs the fruitful Maia's bed,
We 'll bring the firft-born of her flowers
To kifs Thy feet and crown Thy head.
To Thee, dread Lamb ! whose love muft keep
The fhepherds more than they the fheep —
To Thee, meek Majefty ! soft King !
Of fimple graces and sweet loves, —
Each of us his lamb will bring,
Each his pair of filver doves."

Does the nightingale fing more sweetly ?

" Sweet bird, that fhuns the noise of folly —
Moft mufical, moft melancholy."

In this new attempt to turn the Mater Speciosa
into Englifh, we have tried, as in other tranflations,
to preserve, as far as poffible, the form and spirit of
the original.   The authorized text of the *Mater
Dolorosa*, being that of the Roman Breviary, comprises ten ftanzas ; while that of the *Mater Speciosa*
has two more, namely, the fifth and eleventh, whose
answering ftanzas therefore muft be looked for in
some other text.

STABAT MATER

(SPECIOSA).

I.

STABAT Mater speciosa,
Juxta fœnum gaudiosa,
    Dum jacebat parvulus ;
Cujus animam gaudentem,
Lactabundam ac ferventem,
    Pertransivit jubilus.

II.

O quam læta et beata,
Fuit illa immaculata
    Mater Unigeniti !
Quæ gaudebat et ridebat
Exultabat, cum videbat
    Nati partum inclyti.

HYMN OF THE JOYS OF MARY.

I.

STOOD the glad and beauteous mother,
By the hay, where, like no other,
    Lay her little Infant Boy :
Through whose soul — rejoicing, yearn-
        ing,
And with love maternal burning —
    Thrilling paffed the lyric joy.

II.

Oh what grace to her allotted,
Bleffed mother and unspotted
    Of the Sole Begotten One !
Who rejoiced with filvery laughter
As fhe gazed exulting, after
    Birth of her Illuftrious Son.

III.

Quis jam eft, qui non gauderet
Chrifti matrem fi videret
  In tanto solatio?
Quis non poffet collætari
Chrifti matrem contemplari
  Ludentem cum filio?

IV.

Pro peccatis suæ gentis,
Chriftum vidit cum jumentis,
  Et algori subditum;
Vidit suum dulcem natum
Vagientem, adoratum,
  Vili diversorio.

V.

Nato Chrifto in præsepe,
Cœli cives canunt læte
  Cum immenso gaudio;
Stabat senex cum puella,
Non cum verbo nec loquela,
  Stupescentes cordibus.

III.

Who is he, would joy not greatly,
If he saw Chrift's mother, lately
　　With such solace happy made?
Who could view without emotion
That fond mother's rapt devotion,
　Playing with her smiling Babe?

IV.

For His people's fins providing,
Chrift fhe saw with cattle biding,
　　And exposed to winter keen:
Saw her Darling Offspring, crying
As an infant, worfhipped, lying
　　In a lodging vile and mean.

V.

O'er that scene surpaffing fable,
Sing they, Chrift born in a ftable,
　　Heavenly hofts with joy immense:
Old men ftood with maidens gazing,
Speechlefs at that fight amazing,
　　In aftonifhment intense.

VI.

Eja Mater, fons amoris,
Me sentire vim ardoris,
    Fac ut tecum sentiam
Fac ut ardeat cor meum
In amatum Chriſtum Deum,
    Ut Sibi complaceam.

VII.

Sanĉta Mater, iſtud agas,
Prone introducas plagas
    Cordi fixas valide.
Tui nati cœlo lapſi,
Jam dignati fœno nasci
    Pœnas mecum divide.

VIII.

Fac me vere congaudere,
Jesulino cohærere,
    Donec ego vixero !
In me ſiſtat ardor tui ;
Puerino fac me frui
    Dum sum in exilio !

VI.

Make me, Mother, fount of loving,
Feel like force of ardor moving,
    That I thus may feel with thee !
Let my heart with love be burning
That, in Chriſt my God discerning,
    I approved of Him may be !

VII.

Do this, Mother, be entreated,
Firmly fix His wounds, repeated
    Each in my heart crucified !
Of thy Son — the Heavenly Stranger,
Deigning birth now in a manger —
    Sufferings with me divide !

VIII.

Make me truly ſhare thy pleasure,
Cleave to Jesus and Him treasure,
    While I live and all the while !
Work in me thy love's completeneſs,
Feaſt me with thy Sweet One's sweetneſs
    To the end of my exile !

IX.

Virgo virginum præclara,
Mihi jam non fis amara,
        Fac me parvum rapere.
Fac ut pulchrum fantem portem,
Qui nascendo vicit mortem,
        Volens vitam tradere.

X.

Fac me tecum satiari,
Nato me inebriari,
        Stans inter tripudio ! *
Inflammatus et accensus
Obstupescit omnis sensus
        Tali de commercio !

XI.

Omnes stabulum amantes
Et pastores vigilantes
        Pernoctantes sociant.

---

* Since *inter* never rules the ablative, Dr. Schaff proposes to read : " ' Stantem in tripudio ! ' referring ' Stantem ' to ' me.' "

IX.

Maid all other maids exceeding,
Be not bitter to my pleading,
 Let me take thy Little One !
Bear the Babe, His sweet smile wooing,
Who in birth wrought death's undoing,
 Giving life when His begun !

X.

Fill me with thy Child's careffes,
Make me, drunk with joy's excefles,
 In thy leaping transport fhare !
Fired and kindled, ftruck with wonder,
Let each sense the power be under
 Of such commerce sweet and rare !

XI.

All who love the ftable, blending
With the watching fhepherds, spending
 All the night, compose one band.

Per virtutem nati tui
Ora ut electi sui
    Ad patriam veniant!

XII.

Fac me nato custodiri
Verbo Dei præmuniri,
    Conservari gratiâ ;
Quando corpus morietur,
Fac ut animæ donetur
    Tui nati visio.

Pray, through ſtrength of His deserving,
His elect, with course unswerving,
　　May attain the heavenly land !

XII.

Let me by thy Son be warded,
By the word of God be guarded,
　　Kept by grace, refused to none !
When my body death hath riven,
Grant that to my soul be given
　　Joyful viſion of thy Son !

OLD GEMS IN NEW SETTINGS.

Old Gems

IN NEW SETTINGS

COMPRISING THE

CHOICEST OF MEDIÆVAL HYMNS

WITH

ORIGINAL TRANSLATIONS

BY

ABRAHAM COLES, M. D., Ph. D.

THIRD EDITION.

NEW YORK
D. APPLETON AND COMPANY
1891

CONTENTS.

URBS CŒLESTIS SYON;

OR,

THE BETTER COUNTRY.

N Trench's " Sacred Latin Poetry " is given a beautiful Cento of ninety-fix lines, descriptive of the Heavenly Zion, taken from the firft part of a long poem of nearly three thousand lines, entitled " *De Contemptu Mundi*," written in the 12th century by Bernard de Morlas, Monk of Cluny, so called to diftinguifh him from his famous contemporary St. Bernard, Abbot of Clairvaux. Of this Cento a new tranflation is here attempted. Prefixed to it are the eight opening lines of the Poem, admonitory of the nearness of Chrift's second coming to judge the world.

Rev. Dr. John Mason Neale, an accomplifhed

scholar of England, juſt deceased, whoſe tranſlations
of various mediæval hymns have met with much and
merited favor, gave a verſion of the larger part of the
above Cento under the title of " The Celeſtial Country," following, as he tells us, the arrangement of
Trench and not that of Bernard.   The great popularity which this attained, as evinced by the numerous
hymns compiled from it — " Jeruſalem the Golden,"
in particular, having found a place, he gratefully ob-
serves, in some twenty hymnals — " led him to think
that a fuller extract from the Latin and a further
tranſlation into Engliſh might not be unaccept-
able."

Whether by this process there was not as much
loſt as gained admits of some doubt.   It set aſide
Trench's labor of love as impertinent or useless.   The
matter of the earlier tranſlation, with which many
had become familiar, could only be found by diligent
search, *disjecta membra poetæ*, scattered everywhere
up and down the later work.   One, however, might
become reconciled to this, provided improvement
always followed; but we think this can hardly be
claimed.   On the contrary, what is added too often

appears crude, or incongruous, or out of place, or of
inferior intereft. For example, we read : —

> " Here, is the warlike trumpet,
> There, life set free from fin,
> When to the laft Great Supper
> The faithful fhall come in ;
> When the heavenly net is laden
> With fifhes many and great,
> (So glorious in its fulness
> And so inviolate.)"

Without access to the original, it would be impoffible to say which is responfible, the author or
the tranflator, for the ftrange groupings contained in
the following verses : —

> " Jefus, the Gem of Beauty,
> True God and Man, they fing,
> The *never-failing* Garden,
> The *ever-*golden Ring,
> The Door, the Pledge, the Hufband,
> The Guardian of the Court,
> The Day-ftar of Salvation,
> The Porter and the Port."

What better is this than a diftracting medley of
names, whose meaning and fitness, so far from being

2

immediately obvious, it is hard to discover even with time and ſtudy.   Certainly, one needs to poſſess a rare nimbleness of fancy to qualify him to overleap such wide spaces as intervene between " the never-failing Garden" and the " ever-golden Ring," thence on from " the Door, the Pledge, the Huſband," to the diſtant and final reſting-place, " the Porter and the Port" (whatever these may be), without longer pauses in the tranſition than the punctuation calls for. The framer of the Çento did well, therefore, we think, in leaving out lines like these, and no advantage has resulted from their reſtoration.

In regard to the extraordinary merit of the original poem — at leaſt that part of it which forms the exordium, wherein an attempt is made to set forth the purity and peace of the heavenly Paradise, by way of contraſt, and for the purpose of throwing into yet bolder and more appalling relief the abounding pollutions and miseries of earth which it is the chief deſign of the poem to present — there can be but one opinion.   Such is Dr. Neale's appreciation of its excellence, that he has " no heſitation in say-

ing that he looks on these verses of Bernard as the
moſt lovely, in the same way that the *Dies Iræ* is
the moſt sublime, and the *Stabat Mater* is the moſt
pathetic, of mediæval poems. They are, he thinks,
even superior to that glorious hymn on the same
subjeɛt, the *De Gloriâ et Gaudiis Paradiſi* of St.
Peter Damiani. So Trench looks upon " the Ode
of Caſimir (the great Latin poet of Poland) *Urit
me Patriæ decor*, which turns upon the same theme,
— the heavenly homeſickness, — with all its claſſical
beauty, as a less real and deep utterance than the
poor Cluniac monk's."

The great and immediate popularity of Neale's
tranſlation, notwithſtanding its defeɛts, is a further
proof, and the moſt concluſive one, perhaps, of all,
that it poſſeſſes the elements of genuine power —
has indeed that imperiſhable principle of lyric life
which fits it to be the interpreter of the human heart
in all ages, in the nineteenth century no less than
the twelfth. It too doubtless owes much to its
theme, which has furniſhed other hymns of great
sweetness beſides those already named. Two in particular are deserving of special mention, — one in

Latin, *Urbs beata Hirusalem*, and one in Englifh,
O Mother dear, Jerusalem.   But the heavenly heart-
ache, with the soul enamored of its home in the
skies, and longing to depart, never, it is safe to say,
found a sweeter or more touching expreffion than in
these lines of Bernard.   In each golden furrow of
verse are scattered in rich profufion the ripe veritable seeds of those immortal flowers that bloom in
Paradise, whence —

> " Gentle gales,
> Fanning their odoriferous wings, dispense
> Native perfumes, and whisper whence they ftole
> Those balmy spoils.   As when to those who sail
> Beyond the Cape of Hope, and now are paft
> Mozambic, off at sea north-eaft winds blow
> Sabean odors from the spicy fhore
> Of Araby the bleft."

We are perpetually reminded, of course, that the
finger is ftill in the body, in which " he groans, being burdened " — " without are fightings and within
are fears " — is a mourning exile, waiting deliver-
ance, fick from deferred hope, not yet permitted to
enter the Land of Promise, but nevertheless in lieu
thereof lifted to the Mount of Vifion, and favored

with ecftatic glimpses that " bring all heaven before
his eyes." No wonder, therefore, his ftrain is a mingled one, by turns exultant and sad ; its rejoicings
full of interjected fighs — suspirations and aspirations
in the same breath. The holy inhabitants seem
almoft " too happy in their happiness ; " it makes the
contraft with the present ftate too great, too painful ;
it even begets doubt, because it seems too much to
expect ; hope is afraid to soar so high. The mind
is described as finking down baffled and overwhelmed
under the preffure of that " far more exceeding and
eternal weight of glory," blinded and overpowered
by the intolerable splendors of the New Jerusalem ;
and we are reminded of that fine outburft of Pindaric
rapture in which " the Bard " of Gray, in like manner dazzled and amazed by the unexpected fight of
England's diftant renown and greatness, exclaims : —

> " But oh, what solemn scenes on Snowdon's height
> Descending flow their glittering fkirts unroll ?
> Vifions of glory, spare my aching fight,
> Ye unborn ages, crowd not on my soul."

Of the hiftory of the original poem, this much is
known. It was written about the year 1145 by

Bernard, a Cluniac monk, as already ſtated, and addreſſed to Peter, his own abbot. Judging from his
writings, he muſt have poſſeſſed a spirit almoſt as
dauntless as Luther's. Apparently actuated by a
righteous zeal to correct some of the ſhocking abuses
which everywhere prevailed to the disgrace of the
Chriſtian name, he in this poem with terrible sever-
ity and with matchless power of sarcasm exposes
and aſſails them, — plainly denounces the ſhameful
greed and venality of the Roman court, corrupt from
the Pope down, where ſimony was openly practiced,
and nothing could be got without money, but any
thing with.   Here is a specimen of his manner : —

> " Si tua nuncia prævenit uncia, surge, sequaris ;
>   Expete limina, nulla gravamina jam verearis:
>   Si datur uncia, ſtat prope gratia Pontificalis ;
>   Sin procul hæc valet, hæc tibi lex manet eſt schola talis."

Money is needed, if that has preceded, rise, follow, and
   enter;
Bars of the gateway removed ſhall be ſtraightway, now fear
   no preventer ;
Give but the penny, then nigh thee is any Pontifical favor ;
Far off or faileth this thing that availeth, thy case is much
   graver.

Such being its character, it is not surprising, perhaps, that it has been a greater favorite with Proteftants than with Catholics, and that during the time of and fince the Reformation editions have multiplied. It was unburied and firft printed at Paris in 1483. Flacius, in a rare work publifhed at Bâle in 1557, (*Varia doctorum, piorumque vivorum de corrupto Ecclefiæ flatu Poemata,*) pp. 247–349, gives it with the title : *Bernhardus Cluniacus de Contemptu Mundi. Ad Petrum Abbatum suum.* It was reprinted in 1597, and again in 1610, and more recently ftill in Wachler's " Annals " in 1820. Daniel in his " Thesaurus Hymnologicus " gives only the firft eight lines under the heading *De Noviffimis.* These opening lines are repeated here to illuftrate the ftructure of the verse, which of itself is one of the curiofities of literature. It is a bold attempt to combine ancient prosody with modern rhyme. Each hexameter line is made to confift of five dactyls and a final trochee, the second and fourth dactylic feet rhyming together, and the trochaic ending rhyming with the corresponding foot of the following line ; or, as it may be otherwise expreffed, it is an example of " leonine

and tailed rhyme, with lines in three parts, between
which a cæsura is not admiſſible." Below we have
sought to represent to the eye these peculiarities of
ſtructure by marks ; and furthermore, have ventured
a continuation of the attempt juſt made, to imitate
the metre in an Engliſh tranſlation rendered as literal
as poſſible. While one would not care to prosecute
it through a long poem, we are persuaded the thing
could be done, and in a manner to make the verse
tolerably readable and effective. The perpendicular
lines of diviſion indicate the three parts — the firſt
two parts containing two dactyls each, the second
and fourth forming a rhyme ; and the third part containing one dactyl and one trochee, the final trochee
forming a double rhyme with that of the next line.

De Novissimis.

' Hōră nŏvīssĭmă, ‖ tēmpŏră pēssĭmă ‖ sūnt ; vĭgĭlēmŭs !
  Ecce! minaciter ‖ imminet Arbiter ‖ ille supremus !
  Imminet, imminet ‖ ut mala terminet ‖ æqua coronet,
  Recta remuneret ‖ anxia liberet, ‖ æthera donet,
  Auferat aspera ‖ duraque pondera ‖ mentia onustæ,
  Sobria muniat ‖ improba puniat ‖ utraque juste,
  Ille piisſimus, ‖ ille gravisſimus, ‖ ecce ! venit Rex !
  Surgat homo reus ! ‖ Inſtat Homo Deus ‖ a Patre Judex."

Of the Last Times.

Lāſt hoŭrs nŏw tōllĭng ăre, ‖ wōrſt tĭmes ŭnrōllĭng ăre ; ‖
  wātch ! thĕre ĭs dāngĕr.
Ló ! in sublímity, ‖ thréatening proxímity, ‖ hóver'th th' Avén-
  ger !
Hóvereth, hóvereth, ‖ évil uncóvereth, ‖ équity crówneth :
Ríght He rewárdeth then, ‖ cómfort affórdeth then, ‖ héirs of
  heaven ówneth ;
Fróm the mind, ónerous ‖ búrdens and pónderous ‖ beáreth He
  líghtly ;
Ríghteous protécteth He, ‖ wícked rejécteth He ‖ bóth alike
  ríghtly ;
Kíng in His clémency ‖ áwful suprémacy ‖ cómeth to gáther —
Mán disentómbing, the ‖ Gód-Man him dóoming, the ‖ Júdge
  from the Fáther.

Surely " there is a pleasure in poetic pains that
poets only know," otherwise it is impoſſible to conceive that human patience could have held out in
the building up of three thousand lines in so difficult
a metre. Like the execution of those pictures in
mosaic, seen in St. Peter's at Rome, which took
from twelve to twenty years to complete, it so far
transcends all modern capabilities, that one is tempted
to class Patience, in its higher manifeſtations at leaſt,

among "the Loft Arts." The author himself seems
to have been filled with wonder at his own performance ; and pioufly acknowledges, that "if he had
not received directly from on high the gift of intelligence, he had not dared to attempt an enterprise
so little adapted to the powers of the human mind."
What was difficult for the author would be tenfold
more difficult for the tranflator, because there hang
upon him numerous clogs from which the other is
free.   Dr. Neale says : — "I have deviated from
my ordinary rule of adopting the measure of the original, because our language, if it could be tortured to
any diftant resemblance of its rhythm, would utterly
fail to give any idea of the majeftic sweetness of the
Latin."   Whether it was neceffary or wise to go to
the other extreme—of ballad plainness and fimplicity
—some may doubt.

The artful character of the verse, which confti-
tuted one of its chief diftinctions, and upon which
the author had beftowed so much labor, was thereby
neceffarily loft, as well as the richness and melody of
its oft-recurring rhymes.   In the tranflation here
given, the writer has sought to preserve "the leo-

nine and tailed rhymes, with the lines in three parts,"
only lengthening the third member so as to make of it
another line, and using anapests instead of dactyls,
as being a kind of verse better suited to the genius
of Englifh prosody,— the dactylic form being seldom
used, because less flowing and pleafing to the ear.
Had it been thought beft that the dactylic hexameter
form fhould be retained, he is hardly prepared to go
the length of Dr. Neale and deny its poffibility.

How far the present tranflator has succeeded it is
of course for others to judge. He admits that if it
were as easy to be faultless as it is to find fault, there
would be no excuse for imperfection. He claims
nothing for his verfion. It is sent forth as a timid
and humble candidate for public favor, but at the
same time not as a mendicant, afking alms and beg-
ging leave to be. If worthless, let it die — in other
words, let nobody read it. So of his other verfions.
The name, " THE BETTER COUNTRY," was chosen
to diftinguifh it from others upon the same theme.
That it will supersede " The Celeftial Country "
is neither expected nor defired.

URBS CŒLESTIS SYON.

HORA noviſſima, tempora peſſima
     sunt ; vigilemus !
Ecce ! minaciter imminet Arbiter
     ille supremus !
Imminet, imminet ut mala terminet
     æqua coronet,
Recta remuneret, anxia liberet,
     æthera donet ;
Auferat aspera duraque pondera
     mentis onuſtæ
Sobria muniat, improba puniat
     utraque juſte.

THE BETTER COUNTRY.

THE laſt of the hours, iniquity towers,
  The times are the worſt, let us vigils
    be keeping!
  Leſt the Judge who is near, and soon
    to appear,
Shall us at His coming find ſlumbering and ſleep-
    ing.
He is nigh, He is nigh! He descends from the ſky
  For the ending of evil, the right's coronation,
The juſt to reward, relief to afford,
  And the heavens beſtow for the saints' habitation :
To lift and unbind grievous weights from the mind,
  To give every man what is juſt and is equal,
To make the good glad, and puniſh the bad,
  To the praise of His juſtice and grace in the sequel.

Ille piiſſimus, ille graviſſimus
                         ecce! venit Rex!
Surgat homo reus! Inſtat Homo Deus
                 a Patre Judex.

    .   .   .   .

Hic breve vivitur, hic breve plangitur
                    hic breve fletur;
Non breve vivere, non breve plangere
                    retribuetur;
O retributio! ſtat brevis actio
                   vita perennis;
O retributio! cœlica manſio
                  ſtat lue plenis;
Quid datur et quibus? æther egentibus
                  et cruce dignis,
Sidera vermibus, optima sontibus,
                  aſtra malignis.
Sunt modò prælia, poſtmodò præmia;
                  qualia? plena,

Moſt clement and dear, moſt juſt and severe,
  Lo! cometh the King in terrible splendor,
Man springs from the sod, and the Man who is God,
  The Judge from the Father, ſtands sentence to
    render.

   .   .   .   .

The life here below so brief is brief woe,
  A brief mortal space for weeping afforded;—
Not briefly to ſigh, then lie down and die,
  Is the life that 's to be hereafter awarded.
O moſt bleſſèd award! the gift of the Lord,
  A life whose long years cannot be computed;
O ſtrange award given! a manſion in heaven
  Aſſigned to the guilty, the sometime polluted.
What 's given, and to whom? In the firmament,
    room
  To the needy and those by the cross worthy
    rendered—
Yea, on Mercy's sweet terms, orbs celeſtial to
    worms,
  To felons the beſt, to the hateful ſtars, tendered.
Now are battles moſt hard; after these the reward.
  Reward of what sort? Reward without meas-
    ure;—

Plena refectio, nullaque paffio,
      nullaque pœna ;
Spe modò vivitur, et Sion angitur
      a Babylone ;
Nunc tribulatio, tunc recreatio,
      sceptra, coronæ ;
Tunc nova gloria pectora sobria
      clarificabit,
Solvet enigmata, veraque sabbata
      continuabit.
Liber et hoftibus, et dominantibus
      ibit Hebræus ;
Liber habebitur et celebrabitur
      hinc jubilæus.
Patria luminis, inscia turbinis
      inscia litis,
Cive replebitur, amplificabitur
      Israëlitis ;

Full refreshment, repose, full exemption from woes,
  No suffering, no pain, only unalloyed pleasure.
Now live we in hope, and Zion must cope
  With Babylon proud and the powers infernal;
Now affliction makes sad, then delight shall make
    glad,
  And there shall be crowns and sceptres supernal.
Then new glory divine on the righteous shall shine,
  And chase from their breasts the darkness that
    paineth,
Chase doubt and chase fear, and enigmas make
    clear—
  The light of true sabbaths, "the rest that re-
    maineth."
All free from the foe and his master shall go
  The Hebrew, whose feet heavy chains now en-
    viron ; —
He henceforth held free shall keep jubilee,
  No more to be bound in affliction and iron.
A Country of light, unacquainted with night,
  Where of tempest and strife nothing breaks the
    deep slumber,
With inhabitants free it replenished shall be —
  Enlarged with true Israelites countless in number.

Patria splendida, terraque florida,
         libera spinis,
Danda fidelibus eft ibi civibus
         hic peregrinis.
Tunc erit omnibus inspicientibus
         ora Tonantis
Summa potentia, plena scientia,
         pax pia sanctis ;
Pax fine crimine, pax fine turbine,
         pax fine rixa,
Meta laboribus, atque tumultibus
         anchora fixa.
Pars mea Rex meus, in proprio Deus
         ipse decore,
Visus amabitur, atque videbitur
         Auctor in ore.
Tunc Jacob Israël, et Lia tunc Rachel
         efficietur,
Tunc Syon atria pulchraque patria
         perficietur

Country splendid and grand, and a flowery land
  That 's free from all thorns and free from all
    dangers,
Is there to be given to the free born of heaven —
  The faithful, who here are now pilgrims and
    ftrangers.
Shall then be unrolled, to all that behold
  The face of the Thunderer, and to such solely,
The utmoft extreme of power supreme,
  Full knowledge, the unutterable peace of the holy :
A peace by the tongue of flander unftung ; [cor,
  A peace without ftorm, without wrangling or ran-
To labors a goal, and to billows that roll
  And tumults a fixed immovable anchor.
My King is my part, God Himself in my heart,
  In His own proper beauty auguft and endearing,
I fhall see and enfhrine and challenge as mine, —
  My Author and Saviour, — before Him appear-
    ing.
Then the Israel of grace fhall Jacob displace,
  And Leah be Rachel in form and affection ;
Then Zion fhall ftand, a beautiful land,
  In all the completeness of God-like perfection.

O bona Patria, lumina sobria
                te speculantur,
Ad tua nomina lumina sobria
                collacrymantur;
Eft tua mentio pectoris unctio,
                cura doloris,
Concipientibus æthera mentibus
                ignis amoris.
Tu locus unicus, illeque cœlicus
                es paradisus,
Non ibi lacryma, sed placidiſſima
                gaudia, risus.
Eft ibi conſita laurus, et inſita
                cedrus hysopo;
Sunt radiantia jaspide mœnia
                clara pyropo:
Hinc tibi sardius, inde topazius,
                hinc amethyftus;
Eft tua fabrica concio cœlica
                gemmaque Chriftus.

O Country moſt dear, our longing eyes here,
  As they view thee afar, with deſire are aching;
At the sound of thy name our hearts are aflame,
  And our eyes are aweary 'twixt weeping and
    waking.
Thy mention brings reſt, is balm to the breaſt,
  Is the cure of our grief, and takes away sadness;
The thinking of thee and the bliss that ſhall be,
  Is a fire of love and a fountain of gladness.
The only place thou that draws our hearts now,—
  Thou Paradise art, thou our blissful Hereafter;
No tears are found there, no sorrow, no care,
  But sereneſt rejoicings and innocent laughter.
There planted are seen, eternally green,
  The laurel and cedar, with the hyſſop low grow-
    ing;
There are walls with the rays of the jasper ablaze,
  With the carbuncle bright, incandescent and
    glowing:
The sardius ſhines there, here the topaz moſt rare,
  Here the beams of the amethyſt with the reſt
    mingle;
To thy fabric belong the heavenly throng,
  The corner-ſtone Chriſt, gem precious and ſingle.

Tu sine littore, tu sine tempore,
                    fons modò rivus,
Dulce bonis sapis, estque tibi lapis
                    undique vivus.
Est tibi laurea, dos datur aurea,
                    sponsa decora,
Primaque Principis oscula suscipis,
                    inspicis ora :
Candida lilia, viva monilia
                    sunt tibi, sponsa,
Agnus adest tibi, Sponsus adest tibi,
                    lux speciosa ;
Tota negocia, cantica dulcia
                    dulce tonare,
Tam mala debita, quàm bona præbita
                    conjubilare.
Urbs Syon aurea, patria lactea,
                    cive decora,
Omne cor obruis, omnibus obstruis
                    et cor et ora.

Without fhore, without time, everlafting, sublime,
  Thou, fountain and ftream late hitherward flowing,
To the good tafteft sweet, living rock at their feet
  That all through the wilderness gladdened their
      going.   [never brown ;
Thine 's the laurel's green crown with its leaf
  Rich dower all golden, fair spouse, is thee given ;
Thine 's the exquifite bliss of the Prince's firft kiss,
  And the fight of His face like a vifion of heaven.
Fair lilies and white, living gems flafhing bright,
  Compose, happy spouse, thy bridal adorning ;
Sits the Lamb by thy fide, and beams on His bride,
  Like the sun when he breaks through the gates
      of the morning ;
Thy whole sweet employ, in triumph and joy,
  Sweet anthems of praise to warble forever ;
Evils merited tell, bleffings granted as well,
  With fhoutings to grace that terminate never.
City golden and bleft, from thy fields' teeming breaft
  Flow rivers ot milk,— fair people, fair dwellings ;
Thou the whole heart doft whelm, such the
      charms of thy realm,
  Choked is the voice with the heart's mighty
      swellings.

Nescio, nescio, quæ jubilatio,
       lux tibi qualis,
Quàm socialia gaudia, gloria
       quàm specialis:
Laude ftudens ea tollere, mens mea
       victa fatiscit;
O bona gloria, vincor; in omnia
       laus tua vicit.
Sunt Syon atria conjubilantia,
       martyre plena,
Cive micantia, Principe ftantia,
       luce serena:
Eft ibi pascua, mitibus afflua,
       præftita sanctis,
Regis ibi thronus, agminis et sonus
       eft epulantis.
Gens duce splendida, concio candida
       veftibus albis
Sunt fine fletibus in Syon ædibus
       ædibus almis;

Confined here below, I pretend not to know
　What forms this rejoicing, the kind of light given,
Nor how lofty the heights of those social delights,
　Nor how special the glory that conftitutes heaven.
These ftriving to raise in an effort of praise,
　My mind overmaftered, lo! fainteth and faileth;
O glory unknown, I am conquered I own,
　Thy superior praise in all things prevaileth.
There are fhoutings and calls in thy echoing halls
　With the martyr hoft full, a glorious mufter,
With the citizen, bright, with the Prince aye in fight,
　Serene evermore with a soft, sacred luftre.
There sweet paftures around for the gentle abound,
　For the saints a dear flock by the water-brooks
　　grazing;
There's the throne of the King, there the palace-
　　walls ring
　With the sound of a multitude feafting and praifing.
Nation glorious and grand, through the conquering
　　hand
　Of the Leader, a hoft in white veftments fhining,
Through the long rolling years they remain with-
　　out tears;　　　　　　　　　　　　　[ing.
　In the dwellings of Zion there is reft from repin-

Sunt fine crimine, sunt fine turbine,
         sunt fine lite,
In Syon ædibus editioribus
         Israëlitæ.
Urbs Syon inclyta, gloria debita
         glorificandis,
Tu bona vifibus interioribus
         intima pandis :
Intima lumina, mentis acumina
         te speculantur,
Pectora flammea spe modò, poftea
         sorte lucrantur.
Urbs Syon unica, manfio myftica,
         condita cœlo,
Nunc tibi gaudeo, nunc mihi lugeo,
         triftor, anhelo :
Te quia corpore non queo, pectore
         sæpe penetro,

Without crime, without ftorm, to mar and deform,
  Without weapons of ftrife, without matter of
      quarrel,
The Israelites bleft in their lofty homes reft, —
  The olive of peace intertwined with the laurel
O illuftrious name, Zion, higheft in fame,
  Whose glory is that to the glorified owing,
Thou doft knowledge dispense to the innermoft
      sense,
  Thy innermoft good thus secretly fhowing.
My innermoft eyes, thus piercing the fkies,
  From the mind's higheft peaks delighted behold
      thee ;
Now my breaft, all on fire with hope and defire,
  Transported expe&ts sometime to enfold thee.
Thou Zion art one, befide thee is none, —
  Upreared in the fkies a myftical dwelling, —
Now in thee I am glad, now in me I am sad,
  I sob and I figh with breaft heaving and swelling.
Since the body's dull clod keeps me back from my
      God,
  Thee to pierce I oft try with spiritual pinion,

Sed caro terrea, terraque carnea,
         mox cado retro,
Nemo retexere, nemoque promere
         suſtinet ore
Quo tua mœnia, quo capitalia
         plena decore;
Opprimit omne cor ille tuus decor,
         O Syon, O pax,
Urbs ſine tempore, nulla poteſt fore
         laus tibi mendax;
O ſine luxibus, O ſine luctibus,
         O ſine lite.
Splendida curia, florida patria,
         patria vitæ!
Urbs Syon inclyta, turris et edita
         littore tuto,
Te peto, te colo, te flagro, te volo,
         canto, saluto;

But earthy flesh, fleshy earth, makes th' attempt
    little worth,
And I quickly fall back to the senses' dominion.
No mortal may dare with his mouth to declare—
    The task were presumptuous and desperate the
      duty —
Where thy walls, how they rise, in what part of the
    skies
Thy capitals shine complete in their beauty.
Thy charms, they weigh down the heart wholly and
    drown,
    O Zion! O Peace beyond all conceiving!
City blest, without time, dear, tranquil, sublime,
    No possible praise can e'er be deceiving.
No delights vain and lewd, and no sorrows intrude,
    No strife with its wasting, its burning and blasting;
Home happy and high, flowery land of the sky,
    Land native to bliss and the life everlasting.
City, seen from afar, where the glorified are,
    On a safe and high shore, lo! thy towers are
      soaring;
Thee I sue, I admire, thee I love, I desire,
    Sing hymns unto thee, and salute thee adoring.

Nec meritis peto, nam meritis ineto
     morte perire,
Nec reticens tego, quod meritis ego
     filius iræ ;
Vita quidem mea, vita nimis rea,
     mortua vita,
Quippe reatibus exitialibus
     obruta, trita.
Spe tamen ambulo, præmia poftulo
     speque fideque,
Illa perennia poftulo præmia
     nocte dieque.
Me Pater optimus atque piiffimus
     ille creavit ;
In lue pertulit, et lue suftulit,
     a lue lavit.
Gratia cœlica suftinet unica
     totius orbis,

Not on merit, but grace, I reſt solely my case,
  For, measured by merit, condemned my condition ;
Not dumb and perverse do I cover the worse —
  ı own I 'm a child of wrath and perdition.
My life 's a life spilt, void of good, full of guilt,
  A life like to death, without vital expreſſions,
Its innocence quenched, from its proper life
      wrenched,
  Deſtroyed by reason of deadly transgreſſions.
Notwithſtanding in hope I walk softly and grope,
  In hope and in faith heavenly guerdons beseeching ;
I trembling and weak, eternal joys seek,
  By night and by day imploring hands reaching.
Our Father above, whose nature is love,
  The beſt and the deareſt, He made and He
      saved me ;
With my vileness He bore, from my vileness He
      tore,
  From my ſin and uncleanness He graciously
      ıaved me.
Grace celeſtial alone, direct from the throne,
  Is the sovereign proviſion of God's own appointing,

Parcere sordibus, interioribus
                 unctio morbis;
Diluit omnia cœlica gratia,
                 fons David undans
Omnia diluit, omnibus affluit
                 omnia mundans;
O pia gratia, celsa palatia
                 cernere præfta,
Ut videam bona, feftaque consona
                 cœlica fefta.
O mea, spes mea, tu Syon aurea,
                 clarior auro,
Agmine splendida, ftans duce, florida
                 perpete lauro,
O bona patria, num tua gaudia
                 teque videbo?
O bona patria, num tua præmia
                 plena tenebo?
Dic mihi, flagito, verbaque reddito
                 dicque, Videbis.

The sordid of soul to save and make whole,
　For inward diseases the potent anointing.
Grace wafhes away all pollution for aye, —
　The Fountain of David, as free as redundant,
Makes pure all within, makes clean from all fin,
　To all alike flows in measure abundant.
O excellent grace! to an excellent place
　Me raise to discern ftately palaces gleaming,
At a diftance, at leaft, see the heavenly feaft
　With holieft mirth and melody teeming.
Thou Zion! O mine, my hope all divine!
　Like gold, but far nobler, t' our dazzled eyes
　　　looming,
Moft brilliant thy hoft, but their Leader 's thy boaft,
　Brave region with laurel perpetually blooming.
O Country moft sweet, fhall my eyes ever greet
　Thy turrets and towers, and know thy enjoy-
　　ments?
O Country moft bleft, e'er in thee fhall I reft,
　Poffess thy rewards and fhare thy employments?
Tell me, I pray, render answer, and say:
　" Thou fhalt hereafter moft surely behold me —
　　　6

Spem solidam gero; remne tenens ero?
      dic, Retinebis.
O sacer, O pius, O ter et amplius
      ille beatus,
Cui sua pars Deus: O miser, O reus
      hâc viduatus.

        BERNARDUS CLUNIACENSIS.

I hope entertain, the thing hoped shall I gain?
  O say : Thou forever ſhalt have, and ſhalt hold
    me.
Advanced to that sphere, O holy, moſt dear,
  O bleſſéd, thrice bleſſéd and bleſſéd forever,
Who with cleaving of heart, chose God for his
    part :
  O wretched, undone, who from this did him
    sever.

BERNARD OF CLUNY. (XII. Century.)

VENI SANCTE SPIRITUS.

ALL lovers of sacred song agree in assigning to this Hymn a very high place. Clichtoveus thinks it is not possible to praise it enough, and finds it easy to believe that the author in writing it was divinely inspired. Trench characterizes it " as the lovelieft of all the Hymns in the whole circle of Latin Sacred Poetry." Nor is it difficult to discover the grounds of so favorable an eftimate.

Rarely has the spirit of prayer been more happily embodied, or " winged for speedier flight." It is the soul on its knees, devoutly receptive, every door thrown open, eager, expectant, looking and longing for the immediate coming of the Celeftial Vifitant, going forth to meet Him, to kiss His feet, to haften His approach, to teftify a holy and grateful welcome, not unmindful, but yet not deterred by the unspeak-

able greatness of the solicited condescenfion, in afking One " whom the heaven of heavens cannot contain," to ftoop to the need and poverty of its low
eftate, affured by the sure word of promise, and encouraged by paft experiences of His faithfulness,
that " whosoever afketh receiveth." Truly, it were
hard to find a serener, sweeter, truer, truftfuller,
terser utterance, where words so few expreffed so
much, making the air mufical, charming the ear with
their soft, plaintive cadences, and penetrating the
heart with the infinuating grace of their prevalent
pleading.

The merits of its metrical ftructure are in keeping
with its other excellences. It has the triplet character of Sequences in general, confifting of five
ftrophes of fix lines of seven syllables, or ten half
ftrophes, the firft and second lines of which rhyme
together, the third rhyming with the corresponding
third line of the following half ftrophe. The translation here given is made to conform to the original
in these as well as in other respects.

A royal authorfhip is claimed for the Hymn. It
is believed to have been written by Robert II. of

France, who at the age of twenty-four, in the year 996, succeeded to his father, Hugh Capet, and reigned thirty-three years. He is described as — *Omnigenæ virtutis alumnus,* —

> " Pieux, jufte, savant, charitable, fidèle,
> De toutes les vertus, quel plus parfait modèle ? "

By the sentence of Pope Gregory V., his firft marriage, which had been to Bertha, his coufin, was diffolved. He was afterwards married to Conftance, surnamed Blanche, daughter of William Count d'Arles & de Provence, a beautiful princess, but proud, capricious, and unbearable, who conducted herself in so ftrange and violent a manner that but for the moderation and wisdom of her hufband the kingdom would have been overturned. Befides being one of the mildeft of sovereigns and the meekeft of men, he is spoken of as one of the moft learned of his time, particularly in mathematics. So charitable was he that he had always a thousand poor under his care, whom he fed. He was addicted to both poetry and mufic, and so fkilled in both of these arts that some of his compofitions are ftill extant and in use. The

following example of magnanimity, more than royal,
is given. A dangerous conspiracy againſt his kingdom and life having been discovered and the authors
arreſted, as the other nobles were aſſembled to con-
demn them to death, he caused them to be enter
tained in a splendid manner, and the next day
admitted them to the Holy Communion ; after which
he set them at liberty, saying, that he could not put
to death those whom Jesus Chriſt had juſt received
at His table. If these few glimpses of his life re-
veal to us the nature of some of his sorrows, the
hymn here given, admitting that he was the author,
ſhows no less clearly, as Trench remarks, the nature
of his consolations.

The Lutheran Form of Ordination prescribes that
the " Veni Sancte Spiritus " be sung at the beginning of that service. In the Romiſh Church it is
sung on Whitsunday and every day throughout the
week till the Sabbath following. From the general
ſlaughter of the Sequences made in the ſixteenth
century, this and three others were the only ones
that escaped.*

* See DIES IRÆ, p. 61.

VENI SANCTE SPIRITUS.

I.

VENI, Sancte Spiritus,
Et emitte cœlitus,
  Lucis tuæ radium.
Veni, pater pauperum,
Veni, dator munerum,
  Veni, lumen cordium.

II.

Consolator optime,
Dulcis hospes animæ,
  Dulce refrigerium.
In labore requies,
In æftu temperies,
  In fletù solatium.

VENI SANCTE SPIRITUS.

I.

COME, O Holy Spirit, come,
And from Thy celeſtial hcme
  Of Thy light a ray impart !
  Come Thou, Father of the poor !
Come Thou, Giver of heaven's ſtore !
  Come Thou, Light of every heart !

II.

Promised Comforter and beſt,
Of the soul the deareſt Gueſt,
  Sweet Refreſhment here below.
Reſt, in labor, to the feet,
Coolness in the scorching heat,
  Solace in the time of woe.

III.

O lux beatiffima!
Reple cordis intima
   Tuorum fidelium.
Sine tuo numine,
Nihil eft in homine,
   Nihil eft innoxium.

IV.

Lava quod eft sordidum,
Riga quod eft aridum,
   Sana quod eft saucium!
Flecte quod eft rigidum,
Fove quod eft frigidum,
   Rege quod eft devium!

V.

Da tuis fidelibus,
In te confidentibus,
   Sanctum septenarium : *
Da virtutis meritum,
Da salutis exitium,
   Da perenne gaudium !

ROBERTUS REX FRANCIÆ,

* The seven gifts of the Spirit.

III.

O moſt bleſſed Light! the heart's
Innermoſt, moſt hidden parts
  Of Thy faithful people, fill!
Not without Thy favor can
Any thing be good in man,
  Any thing that is not ill.

IV.

What is sordid make Thou clean,
What is dry make moiſt and green,
  What is wounded heal for aye.
Bend what's rigid to Thy will,
Warm Thou whatsoe'er is chill,
  Guide what's devious and aſtray.

V.

To Thy faithful given be —
Those confiding ſtill in Thee —
  Graciouſly the holy seven:
Give Thou virtue's recompense,
Give a safe departure hence,
  Give th' eternal joy of heaven.

ROBERT II. OF FRANCE.
(Beginning of XI. Century.)

VENI CREATOR SPIRITUS.

HIS well-known Hymn, older than the "Veni Sancte Spiritus," is of the same pure type, both being happily characterized by a moſt unromiſh catholicity that makes them sweetly acceptable to all Chriſtian hearts. Here, at leaſt, there is no profane admixture of borrowed or imitated paganism — no ſtanding in the old Roman Pantheon, with a retention of not a little of the form and spirit of the old worſhip, paying vows to manifold apotheoſized Chriſtian saints, as once to deceased pagan heroes or mythological divinities — but a solemn address and devout prayer to that "Creator Spirit," who, in the sublime language of Milton, —

"from the firſt
Was present, and with mighty wings outspread

> Dove-like sat brooding on the vaſt abyss
> And made it pregnant " —

" the third subſiſtence of the divine infinitude, illu-
minating Spirit, the joy and solace of created things ; "
" who can enrich with all utterance and knowledge,
and sends out His Seraphim with the hallowed fire
of His altar, to touch and purify the lips of whom
He pleases ; " the third person of " the One tri-
personal Godhead " —

> " that doth prefer,
> Before all temples, th' upright heart and pure," —

not invoked as a Muse to inspire the poet's song and
bear him upward on the wings of a swift rapture to
" the higheſt heaven of invention," — but as the
indispensable Begetter of a new spiritual life in the
loſt soul of man ; the Finger of the mighty power
of God whose saving and converting touch, reaching
to the deepeſt springs of human thought, feeling, and
conduct, uplifts to the serene altitude of " heavenly
places in Chriſt Jesus ; " the myſtery of an ineffable
Cause, working effectually " to will and to do " in
perfect harmony with the utmoſt moral freedom of

action and volition ; the supreme Gift, and the infinite Giver of gifts ; the refident Paraclete, domefticated in human consciousness ; the Light of a fteady illumination, and the Fire of a continual joy ; the incredible sweetness of whose comforting and compensatory presence and perpetual indwelling, according to the marvelous saying of the Divine Lord Himself, making it expedient that He fhould go away in order that there might follow this fubftituted and surpaffing bleffedness to His bereaved and orphaned disciples when deprived of His own fight and society ; — the Promise of the Father, Proceeding Spirit, manifefted in a miraculous outpouring of baptismal fullness on the day of Pentecoft, as a crowning proof to all, that He whom the Jews had crucified had indeed paffed into the higheft heaven and been to " the right hand of God exalted," thence to dispense this immeasurable grace to the children of men, that they in turn might celebrate in glad doxologies the triune Jehovah, Father, Son, and Holy Ghoft, throughout all ages, Amen !

Although it is not certainly known that Charlemagne is the author, he is commonly so reputed.

Others think the probabilities are in favor of Gregory
the Great. They say, the claffic metre with the in-
termingling rhymes, and the ftyle generally, are Gregory's. So, too, the claffic scanfion of the fifth line
making the penult of "Paraclītus" long, betrays, it is
argued, the Grecian which Gregory was, and Charlemagne was not. On the other hand, it is afferted
that Charlemagne was quite equal to the tafk. " His
eloquence," says his Secretary, "was abundant. He
was able to express with facility all he wifbed ; and
not content with his mother tongue, he beftowed
great pains upon foreign languages. He had taken
so well to the Latin, that he was able to speak pub-
licly in that language almoft as eafily as in his own.
He underftood Greek and ftudied Hebrew." He
wrote other verses, which are ftill extant : — an epi-
taph on Adrian I., the Song of Roland, an ode to
the scholar Warnefride, and an epigram in hexameter
verse. There exifts a letter addreffed by him to his
bifhops, entitled *De gratiâ septiformis Spiritus*, fhowing that he took a special intereft in the subject of
the Hymn. Moreover, the twofold proceffion of
the Holy Ghoft, affirmed in the fixth ftrophe, and

with an emphafis implying that it was confidered an important article of belief, was firft confirmed as the doctrine of the Weftern Church by a Synod affembled under imperial auspices at Aix-la-Chapelle in the year 809; and this circumftance ftrengthens, it is thought, the probability that he was the author. Charlemagne, " claimed by the Church as a saint, by the French as their greateft king, by the Germans as their countryman, by the Italians as their emperor," died at Aix-la-Chapelle, we are told, with his crown upon his head, and his copy of the Gospels upon his knees.

Befides being used as a Pentecoftal Hymn, it has been the cuftom to employ it on great occafions like the coronation of kings, the celebration of synods, and, in the Romifh Church, the creation of popes, &c. It is the only Breviary Hymn retained by the Episcopal Church, where a place is affigned it in the offices for the ordination of priefts and the consecration of bifhops. The Prayer Book contains two verfions. Dryden's admirable paraphrase is well known. The rendering here given is much more close. In German there are several tranflations.

One by Luther begins : *Kum Schepher heiliger Geift.*

The Latin text varies in different editions. Some interpolate between the 5th and 6th verses the following additional one :

> Da gaudiorum præmia,
> Da gratiarum munera,
> Diffolve litis vincula,
> Adftringe pacis fœdera.

The final verse is sometimes given thus :

> Sit laus Patri cum Filio,
> San&to fimul Paraclito,
> Nobisque mittat Filius,
> Charisma San&ti Spiritus.

That the final verse was added afterwards may be deduced from the fact that the quantity of " Paraclito " in this differs from that of " Paraclitus " in the second verse of the hymn — the penult in the one case being fhort and in the other long. The Hymn moreover in its present form has, so to speak, a double doxology or celebration of the Trinity, which increases the probability that it ended originally with the fixth verse.

VENI CREATOR SPIRITUS.

I.

VENI, Creator Spiritus,
Mentes tuorum vifita,
Imple superna gratia,
Quæ tu creafti pectora.

II.

Qui Paraclitus diceris
Donum Dei altiffimi,
Fons vivus, ignis, charitas,
Et spiritalis unctio.

III.

Tu septiformis munere,[1]
Dextræ Dei tu digitus,[2]
Tu rite promiffum Patris,
Sermone ditans guttura.

VENI CREATOR SPIRITUS.

I.

REATOR Spirit, Gueſt Divine,
Come, viſit and inhabit Thine,
Enter the mind's Moſt Holy Place,
And breaſts Thou madeſt fill with grace.

II.

Thou who art called the Paraclete,
Of God Moſt High the Gift complete,
The Living Fount, the Fire, the Love,
And Holy Unction from above.

III.

Sevenfold the gifts at Thy command,
Finger of God's supreme right hand,
The Promise of the Father, who
Doſt throats enrich with utt'rance new.

IV.

Accende lumen senfibus,
Infunde amorem cordibus,
Infirma noftri corporis,
Virtute firmans perpeti.

V.

Hoftem repellas longius,
Pacemque dones protinus :
Ductore fic te prævio
Vitemus omne noxium.

VI.

Per te sciamus da Patrem
Noscamus atque Filium,
Teque utriusque Spiritum
Credamus omni tempore.

VII.

Deo Patri fit gloria,
Et Filio, qui a mortuis
Surrexit, ac Paraclito,
In sæculorum sæcula.

CAROLUS MAGNUS.

IV.

Kindle the senses, light impart,
Infuse Thy love in every heart,
Weaken our body's bent to wrong,
In lafting virtue making ftrong.

V.

Drive farther· off the hellifh foe,
And conftant peace henceforth beftow.
May we — Thou, Leader in the way —
All evil fhun, nor go aftray.

VI.

Grant we may know in verity
The Father and the Son through Thee;
And in all time may Thee believe
Spirit of Both, and so receive.

VII.

Be God the Father glorified,
And God the Son who for us died
And rose, and God the Paraclete,
Ages on ages infinite.

CHARLEMAGNE.   (Beginning of IX. Century.)

[1] The seven gifts of the Holy Spirit (Isaiah xi. 2, 3) are: 1. Wisdom (*sapientia*); 2. Underſtanding (*intellectus*); 3. Counsel (*conſilium*); 4. Fortitude (*fortitudo*); 5. Knowledge (*scientia*); 6. Piety (*pietas*); 7. Fear of the Lord (*timor*). Whence the verse : —

> *Sap. intel. con. for. sci. pi. ti. collige dona.*

[2] The title here given to the Holy Ghoſt — *Digitus Dei* — borrowed from Luke xi. 20, and answering to the *Spiritus Dei* of Matthew xii. 28, is adapted, so it is thought, to ſuggeſt other ideas beſides the ſingle one of power. As the fingers are various but have a common origin in the hand, so there are diverſities of gifts and operations, but the same Spirit. Notwithſtanding diviſions, there is a root of unity. Jerome finds in it moreover a hint of the homoouſian union of the Spirit with the Father and the Son. "If, therefore," he argues, "the Son is the hand and arm of God, and the Holy Ghoſt His finger, there is one ſubſtance of the Father, Son, and Holy Ghoſt." It is ſtated in Exodus that "the Lord delivered unto Moses two tables of ſtone written with the finger of God;" and Paul speaks of the Corinthian converts as "epiſtles of Chriſt, written not with ink, but the Spirit of the living God : not in tables of ſtone, but in the fleſhly tables of the heart," — thus furniſhing another illuſtration of scriptural usage in aſcribing the same function and work to the finger of God and the Spirit of God.

ALPHABETIC JUDGMENT-HYMN.

(HYMNUS ALPHABETICUS DE DIE JUDICII.)

HE venerable Bede, an Englifh monk, who lived in the seventh century, makes mention of this Alphabetical Hymn, so that it muft have been written before his time. The author is unknown. Daniel remarks: "It is interefting to compare this piece on the Laft Judgment with that moft celebrated one, *Dies iræ, dies illa*, by which in majefty and terror, not in holy fimplicity and truthfulness, it is surpaffed." Neale, likewise, speaking of this Hymn, says: "It manifeftly contains the germ of the *Dies Iræ*, to which, however inferior in lyric fervor and effect, it scarcely yields in devotion and fimple realization of the subject."

HYMNUS DE DIE JUDICII.

PPAREBIT repentina Dies Magna
    Domini
Fur obscura velut nocte improvisos oc-
    cupans,
B revis totus tum parebit prisci luxus sæculi,
    Totum fimul cum clarebit præterifle sæculum.
C langor tubæ per quaternas terræ plagas concinens,
    Vivos una mortuosque Chrifto ciet obviam.
D e cœlefti Judex arce, majeftate fulgidus
    Claris angelorum choris comitatus aderit :
E rubescet orbis lunæ, sol et obscurabitur,
    Stella cadent pallescentes, mundi tremet ambitus ;
F lamma, ignis anteibit jufti vultum Judicis,
    Cœlos, terras et profundi fluctus ponti devorans.
G loriosus in sublimi Rex sedebit solio,
    Angelorum tremebunda circumftabant agmina,

JUDGMENT–HYMN.

S a thief in the night, when none waketh
    to ward,
  Shall be the surprise of that Day of the
    Lord ;
B rief ſhall then seem all its pomp and display
  When the world ſhall have paſſed and its faſhion
    away.
C langor of trumpet-call, everywhere spread,
  Shall gather to Chriſt all the quick and the dead.
D azzling from heaven the Judge ſhall descend,—
  Bright choirs of angels His coming attend :
E ’en as blood ſhall the moon be, the sun it ſhall
    fade,
  Stars paling ſhall fall, and the world be afraid ;
’F ore the face of the Judge, lo ! a fire ſhall sweep
  Devouring the heavens, the land and the deep.
G lorious the King ſhall be seated on high,
  While trembling around ſtand the hoſts of the
    ſky.

H ujus omnes ad electi colligentur dexteram,
   Pravi pavent a siniftris hœdi velut fœtidi :
I te, dicit Rex ad dextros, regnum cœli sumite,
   Pater vobis quod paravit ante omne sæculum,
C aritate qui fraterna me juviftis pauperem,
   Caritatis nunc mercedem reportate divites.
L æti dicent : quando, Chrifte, pauperem te vidimus,
   Te, Rex magne, vel egentem miserati juvimus :
M agnus illis dicet Judex : cum juviftis pauperes,
   Panem, domum, veftem dantes, me juviftis
      humiles.
N ec tardabit et siniftris loqui juftus Arbiter :
   In Gehennæ maledicti flammas hinc discedite ;
O bsecrantem me audire despexiftis mendicum,
   Nudo veftem non dediftis, neglexiftis languidum.
P eccatores dicent : Chrifte, quando te vel pauperem,
   Te, Rex magne, vel infirmum contemnentes
      sprevimus.
Q uibus contra Judex altus : mendicanti quamdiu
   Opem ferre despexiftis, me spreviftis improbi.

H is elect on the right fhall be gathered, the while
On His left fhall be placed the wicked and vile ;
" I nherit the kingdom " — fhall the King say to
those —   [was ;
" The Father prepared for you ere the world
" K indly, Me poor, ye did succor in love,
" Love's guerdon receive now, ye rich, from
above."
" L ord," they fhall say, " when did we e'er see
" Thee poor, and in want gave succor to
Thee ? "
" M e " — fhall He say — " ye did succor, 't was I
" When ye cared for the poor, fhared the timely
supply."
N ext, over the left, in loud thunders fhall burft :
" To the flames of Gehenna depart ye accurft :
" O n Me needy ye looked and turned a deaf ear,
" When naked Me clothed not, when fick
came not near."
" P ray tell us, Great King, when, poor or forlorn,
" Did we ever contemn Thee or treat Thee
with scorn ? "
Q ueftioned, the Judge fhall then anfwer : "Know ye
" What time ye the needy despised ye did Me."

R etro ruent tum injufti ignes in perpetuos,
   Vermis quorum non morietur, flamma nec reftin-
      guitur,
S atan atro cum miniftris quo tenetur carcere,
   Fletus ubi mugitusque, ftrident omnes dentibus.
T unc fideles ad cœleftem suftollentur patriam,
   Choros inter angelorum regni petent gaudia,
U rbis summæ Hirusalem introibunt gloriam
   Vera lucis atque pacis in qua fulget vifio.
X PM regem jam paterna claritate splendidum
   Ubi celsa beatorum contemplantur agmina —
Y dri fraudes ergo cave, infirmantes subleva,
   Aurum temne, fuge luxus fi vis aftra petere,
Z ona clara caftitatis lumbos nunc præcingere,
   In occursum Magni Regis fer ardentes lampades.

R ufh fhall the wicked then, plunged in the fire
Where the worm fhall not die nor the flame
fhall expire.
S atan in chains fhall there hold them beneath,
Where are weeping and wailing and gnafhing of
teeth.
T hen the faithful, upborne to the heavenly land,
Shall partake of the joys at Jehovah's right hand ;
U fhered fhall be in that Salem above
Where fhines the true vifion of light, peace, and
love ;
'**X** alted as King, in divinity dreft,
There Chrift fhall be viewed by the hofts of the
bleft.
Y ou the Serpent's wiles fhun, you the weak ones
fuftain,
Scorn gold, flee excess, would you the ftars gain.
Z one of chaftity bright be your girdle, forth bring
Your lamps trimmed and burning to meet the
Great King.

UNKNOWN AUTHOR.
(VII. Century, or earlier.)

ON CONTEMPT OF THE WORLD.

(CARMEN JACOPONI DE CONTEMPTU MUNDI.)

THIS Hymn was firſt printed in Paris, 1496. It has been ascribed to various persons, among the reſt to St. Bernard ; also to Walter Mapes, Archdeacon of Oxford, England, who lived in the twelfth or thirteenth century. But Wadding, in his " Annals of the Minorites," points to Jacopone as the true author of this as well as of the *Stabat Mater ;* and this now would seem to be the received opinion. Du Meril collates the third and fourth verses with the following lines taken from another part of the same poem as " The Better Country," — Bernard's " De Contemptu Mundi." The reader will readily recognize the rhyming hexameter with which he was made familiar in the former extraƈt :

" Eſt ubi gloria nunc, Babylonia ? sunt ubi durus
Nabuchodonozor et Darii vigor, illeque Cyrus ?
Nunc ubi curia pompaque Iulia ?   Cæsar obiſti ;
Te truculentior, orbe potentior ipse fuiſti.
Nunc ubi Marius atque Fabricius inscius auri ?
Mors ubi nobilis et memorabilis aℸtio Pori ?
Diva philippica, vox ubi cœlica nunc Ciceronis ?
Pax ubi civibus atque rebellibus ira Catonis ?
Nunc ubi Regulus, aut ubi Romulus, aut ubi Remus ?
Stat rosa priſtina nomine, nomina nuda tenemus."

Here is more in the same vein, occurring in a
hymn " On Death," of an uncertain date and by an
unknown author:

" Ubi Plato, ubi Porphyrius ;
   Ubi Tullius aut Virgilius ;
   Ubi Thales, ubi Empedocles,
   Aut egregius Ariſtoteles ;
   Alexander ubi rex maximus ;
   Ubi Heℸor Troiæ fortiſſimus ;
   Ubi David rex doℸtiſſimus,
   Ubi Salomon prudentiſſimus ;
   Ubi Helena Parisque roseus ;
   Ceciderunt in profundum ut lapides :
   Quis scit, an detur eis requies."

DE CONTEMPTU MUNDI.

I.

UR mundus militat sub vana gloria,
Cujus prosperitas eſt tranſitoria?
Tam cito labitur ejus potentia,
Quam vasa figuli, quæ sunt fragilia.

II.

Plus crede literis scriptis in glacie,
Quam mundi fragilis vanæ fallaciæ!
Fallax in præmiis virtutis specie,
Quæ nunquam habuit tempus fiduciæ.

III.

Dic, ubi Salomon, olim tam nobilis,
Vel ubi Sampson eſt, dux invincibilis?

I.

HY toileth the world in the service of
  glory,
Whose triumphs are brief, though the
  proudeſt in ſtory?
Its power is, though high as the heart ever flattered,
Like the vase of the potter, that quickly is ſhattered.

II.

Truſt a pledge writ in ice when winter is leaving —
Than the world's fair falsehoods less vain and
  deceiving!
Moſt false in its promise of virtue's rewarding,
The time of redemption it never regarding.

III.

O say, where is Solomon, aforetime so glorious?
Or where now is Sampson, a leader victorious?

Vel pulcher Absalom, vultu mirabilis,
Vel dulcis Jonathas, multum amabilis?

IV.

Quo Cæsar abiit, celsus imperio?
Vel Xerxes splendidus, totus in prandio?
Dic ubi Tullius, clarus eloquio?
Vel Ariftoteles, summus ingenio?

V.

Tot clari proceres, tot rerum spatia,
Tot ora præsulum, tot regna fortia,
Tot mundi principes, tanta potentia,
In ictu oculi clauduntur omnia.

VI.

Quam breve feftum eft hæc mundi gloria!
Ut umbra hominis, fic ejus gaudia,
Quæ femper subtrahunt æterna præmia,
Et ducunt hominem ad dura devia.

Or beautiful Absalom, of wondrous appearing?
Or Jonathan sweet, exceeding endearing?

IV.

Where 's Cæsar gone now, in command high and
    able?
Or Xerxes the splendid, complete in his table?
Or Tully, with powers of eloquence ample?
Or Aristotle, of genius the higheſt example?

V.

So many great nobles, things, adminiſtrations,
So many high chieftains, so many brave nations,
So many proud princes, and power so splendid,
In a moment, a twinkling, all utterly ended.

VI.

Earth's glory how vain, a brief banquet its meas-
    ure!
As is a man's ſhadow even so is its pleasure,
Which forever of endless rewards makes deduction,
And leads in the hard devious paths of deſtruction.

VII.

O esca vermium, O maſſa pulveris,
O ros, O vanitas, cur ſic extolleris ?
Ignoras penitus, utrum cras vixeris ;
Benefac omnibus, quamdiu poteris !

VIII.

Hæc mundi gloria, quæ magni penditur,
Sacris in literis flos fœni dicitur ;
O leve folium, quod vento rapitur !
Sic vita hominis hac via tollitur.

IX.

Nil tuum dixeris, quod potes perdere !
Quod mundus tribuit, intendit rapere.
Superna cogita ! cor ſit in æthere !
Felix, qui potuit mundum contemnere !

JACOBUS DE BENEDICTIS.

VII.

O food for the worms, O mass of duſt drifted,
O dew, O vanity, why so uplifted?
Thou know'ſt not at all, if thou 'lt live till to-
    morrow ;
Do good while thou canſt to the children of sorrow!

VIII.

This glory of earth, which is much eſtimated,
As the flower of grass is in Holy Writ rated:
O leaf light and frail, by the wind snatched and
    harried!
Ev'n so human life is away from earth carried.

IX.

Call nought then thine own which is loſt ere one
    knoweth!
Earth meaneth to take the good it beſtoweth:
On supernal joys think! let thy heart be in heaven!
Contemn thou the world, and beware of its leaven!
JACOPONE. (XIII. Century.)

WORKS

OF

ABRAHAM COLES,

REVIEWED BY

EMINENT CRITICS.

WORKS OF ABRAHAM COLES, M.D. LL.D.

LATIN HYMNS, in Four Parts, viz.:
  I.   DIES IRÆ, in Thirteen Original Versions. Sixth edition. (1891.)
  II. STABAT MATER (Dolorosa). Third edition.
  III. STABAT MATER (Speciosa). Second edition.
  IV. OLD GEMS IN NEW SETTINGS. Third edition.

> All bound together, with biographical and critical prefaces, with full-page illustrations of: "The Last Judgment," by Michael Angelo; "Christus Remunerator," "St. Augustine and His Mother," "Faith and Hope," by Ary Scheffer; "Mary at the Cross," by Paul Delaroche; Raphael's "Madonna di San Sisto," the gem of the Dresden gallery; "Ecstasy and Prayer," by Ch. Landelle; etc., etc. Crown, 8vo, pp. 249. $3.00.

THE MICROCOSM AND OTHER POEMS.

> Including three additional versions of the "Dies Iræ," National Lyrics, and Hymns for Children. Beautifully illustrated. Crown, 8vo, pp. 348. $2.50.

THE LIFE AND TEACHINGS OF OUR LORD.
In verse.

> Being a complete, harmonized exposition of the four gospels, with original notes, etc. A cyclopædia of religious knowledge. Two volumes in one.
>
> Illustrated with Munkacsy's "Christ Before Pilate." Crown, 8vo, pp. 800. $2.50.

THE LIFE AND TEACHINGS OF OUR LORD.
In verse.   Two volumes, viz.:

Vol. I.   THE EVANGEL.

Illustrated with twenty-eight full-page "artotype" copies of: "Ecce Homo," by Guido Reni; "The Four Evangelists," by Thorwaldsen; "Salvator Mundi," by Carlo Dolce; "The First Death," by Adrian V. Werff; "The Annunciation," by Prof. E. Deger; "The Visitation," by Bida; "Golgotha," by J. L. Gerome; "La Notte," by Correggio; "The Presentation in the Temple," by W. T. C. Dobson; "The Magi Going to Bethlehem," by J. Portaels; "The Flight into Egypt," by Dorothea Lister; "The Massacre of the Innocents," by Guido; "The Shadow of the Cross," by Phil. R. Morris; "Nazareth," by W. T. C. Dobson; "The Good Shepherd," by Murillo; "The Finding of the Saviour in the Temple," by W. Holman Hunt; "The Voice in the Wilderness," by Guido Reni; "Jesus, the Christ," by Ary Scheffer; "The Scapegoat," by W. Holman Hunt; "The Temptation," by Ary Scheffer; "Christus Consolator," by Ary Scheffer; "The Holy Family," by F. Ittenbach; "Christ's Mother and Brethren," by Bida; "The Marriage at Cana," by Paul Veronese; "Christ by the Sea of Galilee," by Bida; "Jeptha's Return," by Leon Glaize; "Ruth and Naomi," by Ary Scheffer; "The Cleansing of the Temple," by Barthelemy Manfredi; "Invocation and Petition," by Ch. Landelle; etc. Crown, 8vo, pp. 405. $3.50.

Vol. II.   THE LIGHT OF THE WORLD.

Illustrated with full-page "artotype" copies of: "Christ Before Pilate," by Munkacsy; "The Good Shepherd," by Dobson; "Christ and His Disciples on Their Way to Emmaus," by B. Plockhorst; etc. Crown, 8vo, pp. 395. $2.50.

A NEW RENDERING OF THE HEBREW PSALMS
INTO ENGLISH VERSE.
>   With notes, critical, historical and biographical, in-
>   cluding an historical sketch of the French, English and
>   Scotch metrical versions.   pp. 300. $1 25.

MAN, THE MICROCOSM.   Fourth (Memorial) edition.   (1891.)
>   With portrait and biographical sketch of the author,
>   and twelve full-page "artotype" illustrations, viz.:
>   "The Transfiguration," Raphael's last and grandest
>   work; "Salvator Mundi," by Carlo Dolce; "Aurora,"
>   by Guido Reni, "the artist's finest work;" "The Last
>   Days of Mozart," from a photograph of the original
>   painting by Kaulbach; "Deerhurst," from photographs,
>   by Edward Bierstadt; music and words; etc. $3.00.

MAN, THE MICROCOSM.   Fifth (Physicians') edition.   (1891.)
>   With portrait and biographical sketch of the author,
>   and illustrated with ten full-page illustrations, viz.:
>   "Ambrose Paré, the Father of French Surgery;" "Ed-
>   ward Jenner, the Discoverer of Vaccination;" "Andreas
>   Vesalius, author of the immortal work, 'De Corporis
>   Humani Fabrica;'" "William Harvey Demonstrating
>   to Charles I, His Theory of the Circulation of the
>   Blood;" Rembrandt's famous "Lesson in Anatomy—
>   Prof. Tulp and His Pupils;" the "Apollo Belvedere,"
>   from a photograph of the original statue; the "Venus
>   de Medici, which from its exquisite proportions and
>   perfection of contour has become the most celebrated
>   standard of female form extant;" "Theodor Billroth
>   and his Clinical Assistants, Vienna;" etc. $2.50.
>   *An appropriate gift to a physician.*

For sale by all booksellers; or sent, at our expense, to
any address, on receipt of price mentioned.

D. APPLETON & CO., Publishers,
Bond street, New York.

CRITICS AND CRITICISMS.

Richard Grant White (1821–1885), in "The Albion":

"We commend the volume, 'Dies Iræ, in Thirteen Original Versions,' as one of great interest; and an admirable tribute from American scholarship and poetic taste to the supreme nobility of the original poem. Dr. Coles has shown a fine appreciation of the spirit and rhythmic movement of the Hymn, as well as unusual command of language and rhyme; and we much doubt whether any translation of the 'Dies Iræ,' better than the first of the thirteen, will ever be produced in English, except perhaps by himself. . . . As to the translation of the Hymn, it is perhaps the most difficult task that could be undertaken. To render 'Faust' or the 'Songs of Egmont' into fitting English numbers, would be easy in comparison."

The Rev. Samuel Irenæus Prime, D. D. (1812–1885), in the "New York Observer":

"The book is a gem both typographically and intrinsically; beautifully printed at the 'Riverside Press,' in the loveliest antique type, on tinted paper, with liberal margins, embellished with exquisite photographs of the great masterpieces of Christian Art, and withal elegantly and solidly bound in Matthew's best style, a gentlemanlike book, suggestive of Christmas and the centre-table; and its contents worthy of their dainty envelope, amply entitling it as well to a place on the shelves of the scholar. . . . . The first two of the thirteen versions of the 'Dies Iræ' appeared in the 'Newark Daily Advertiser' as long ago as 1847. They were extensively copied by the press, and warmly commended—particularly by the Rev. Drs. James W. Alexander and W. R. Williams, scholars whose critical acumen and literary ability are universally recognized—as being the best of the English versions in double rhyme; and examples of singular success in a difficult undertaking, in which many, and of eminent name, had been competitors. The eleven other versions are worthy companions of those which have received such eminent endorsement. Indeed, we are not sure but that the last, which is in the same measure as Crashaw's, but in our judgment far superior, will please the general taste most of all."

William Cullen Bryant (1794–1878), in the New York "Evening Post":

"There are few versions of the Hymn which will bear to be compared with these; we are surprised that they are all so well done."

James Russell Lowell (1819–1891), in "The Atlantic Monthly":

"Dr. Coles has made, we think, the most successful attempt at an English translation of the Hymn that we have ever seen. . . . . He has done so well that we hope he will try his hand on some of the other Latin Hymns. By rendering them in their own metres, and with so large a transfusion of their spirit as characterizes his present attempt, he will be doing a real service to the lovers of that kind of religious poetry in which neither the religion nor the poetry is left out. He has shown that he knows the worth of faithfulness."

"Christian (Quarterly) Review :"

"Of Dr. Coles' remarkable success as respects these particulars (namely, faithfulness and variety), no one competent to judge can doubt. . . . For all that enters into a good translation, fidelity to the sense of the original, uniform conformity to its tenses, preservation of its metrical form without awkwardly inverting, inelegantly abbreviating, or violently straining the sense of the words, and the reproduction of its vital spirit—for all these qualities Dr. Coles' first translation stands, we believe, not only unsurpassed, but unequalled in the English language."

"The Boston Transcript" says:

"The 'Dies Iræ' is by far the most interesting hymn to Protestants and poets, of all that our fathers used to sing or hear in a strange tongue ' not understanded of the people;' and so thoroughly has the translator (Dr. Coles) entered the circle of the old song's heat and strength that he has been carried through it again and again, and here are more than a dozen versions of the same Latin words, and an historical criticism in a strong, earnest and poetical style akin to that of the hymn itself."

Lady Jane Franklin, wife of Sir John Franklin, when in this country, met Dr. Coles at the residence of a mutual friend; similarity of tastes, and the interest taken by Dr. Coles in the search for her husband, ripened the acquaintanceship into that of friendship. From her letter written from New York, October 22d, 1860, we quote the following :

"Dr. Abraham Coles:

"Dear Sir—I cannot deny myself the pleasure of thanking you

once more for your most beautiful little book, 'The Dies Iræ, in Thirteen Original Versions,' which I value not only for its intrinsic merit, but as an expression of your very kind feelings towards me. Believe me, gratefully and truly yours."

William C. Prime, in the "Journal of Commerce":

"Dr. A. Coles has long been known to the literary world as specially successful in the translation of Latin Hymns. His renderings of the 'Dies Iræ' are familiar to many readers. He has now also prepared a book entitled 'Old Gems in New Settings,' an exquisite volume, in which we find the 'De Contemptu Mundi,' the 'Veni Sancte Spiritus, and other fine old favorites skillfully and gracefully translated. The grand hymn or poem of Bernard de Clugny, of which the extracts in this book are styled 'Urbs Cœlestis Syon,' is rendered in a style very nearly resembling the original, and gives the reader, who does not understand Latin, an excellent idea of the peculiar characteristics of the hymn of Bernard. Besides these, we have the 'Stabat Mater,' with a complete history of the noble hymn, and a very fine translation. The lovers of old hymns owe a special debt of gratitude to Dr. Coles for the good taste and the thorough appreciation and ability which he brings to the work of placing these glorious old songs within reach of the modern world. We could wish them to become favorites in every family, and they will so become in spite of their Latin origin."

The Rev. Philip Schaff, D. D., LL. D., in "Hours at Home":

"There are about eighty German translations of the 'Stabat Mater' and several English translations. But very few of the latter strictly preserve the original metre. The English double rhyme rarely expresses the melody and pathos of the Latin. Dr. Abraham

Coles, the well-known author of fourteen translations of 'Dies Iræ,'
has probably best succeeded in a faithful rendering of the 'Mater
Dolorosa.' * * * The admirable English version of the 'Mater
Dolorosa,' which carefully preserves the measure of the original,
is from Dr. Coles, who kindly granted us permission to use it."

"The Republican," Springfield, Mass.:

"Dr. Abraham Coles won fame, and sure fame, by the most
poetic and truthful translations ever given of that great mediæval
hymn, the 'Dies Iræ.'"

George Ripley (1802–1880), in the "New York Tribune":

"United with a rare command of language and facility of versification, this is the secret of the eminent success with which the
translator has reproduced the solemn litany of the Middle Ages in
such a variety of forms. If not all of equal excellence, it is hard to
decide as to their respective merits, so admirably do they embody
the tone and sentiment of the original in vigorous and impressive
verse. The essays which precede and follow the Hymn, exhibit the
learning and the taste of the translator in a most favorable light,
and show that an antiquary and a poet have not been lost in the
study of science and the practice of a laborious profession. In
addition to the thirteen versions of 'Dies Iræ,' the volume contains
translations of the 'Stabat Mater,' 'Urbs Cœlestis Syon,' 'Veni
Creator Spiritus,' and other choice mediæval hymns which have
been executed with equal unction and felicity.

"We have also a poem by the same author, entitled 'The Microcosm,' read before the Medical Society of New Jersey at its centenary
anniversary. It is an ingenious attempt to present the principles
of the animal economy in a philosophical poem, somewhat after
the manner of Lucretius, and combining scientific analysis with

religious sentiment. In ordinary hands, we should not regard this
as a happy, nor a safe experiment, but the dexterity with which it
has been managed by Dr. Coles, illustrates his versatile talent as
well as the originality of his conceptions.

The Rev. James McCosh, D. D., LL. D., President
of the College of New Jersey, in a letter to Dr. Coles :

"I have read with the liveliest delight your translations of the
'Latin Hymns.' I wonder how you could have drawn out thirteen
of the 'Dies Iræ,' all in the spirit and manner of the original, and
yet so different. I thought each the best as I read it. * * * *
I have read enough of 'The Microcosm' to see that it is thoroughly
scientific."

Richard Stockton Field, LL. D., (1803–1870), in 1838
Attorney General of New Jersey; in 1862 United States
Senator; in 1863 appointed by President Lincoln United
States District Judge for the District of New Jersey; at
the time of his death President of the New Jersey His-
torical Society:

"PRINCETON, N. J.
"DR. ABRAHAM COLES :
"MY DEAR SIR—With the original 'Dies Iræ' and 'Stabat
Mater' I have long been familiar. They have always had a peculiar charm, I may say fascination, about them, and I have loved to
repeat them. And now I have no hesitation in saying that they
never have been, and I doubt if they ever will be, as well translated
into English verse as they are in your volume.
"Knowing the difficulty of the task, seeing how others have

failed. I am indeed astonished at your success. With the strictest
fidelity, your translations have all the tenderness, pathos and
rhythm of the beautiful and touching originals. I speak more
particularly of the first of the ' Dies Iræ' and of the 'Stabat Mater.'
The two first stanzas of the latter are perfect.

"Your 'Microcosm,' too, is a noble poem. It has many strik-
ingly beautiful passages. It evinces science and culture, and poetical talent of high order. You display great command of language,
and great facility of versification. Your prose also is easy and
graceful. I am glad of the opportunity afforded me of rendering
this feeble tribute to their merits. Very truly yours."

The "Newark Daily Advertiser :"

"Dr. Coles has supplied a want and done a graceful work in
"The Microcosm." What the flower or babbling stream is to Words-
worth, that is the stranger, more complex, and more beautiful human
frame to our author. In its organs, its powers, its aspirations, and
its passions, he finds ample theme for song. . . Everywhere the
rhythm is flowing and easy, and no scholarly man can peruse the
work without a glance of wonder at the varied erudition, classical,
poetical, and learned, that crowds its pages, and over-flows in foot-
notes. And through the whole is a devout religious tone and a
purity of purpose worthy of all praise."

Edmund C. Stedman:

"Dr. Coles' researches, made so lovingly and conscientiously in
his special field of poetical scholarship, have given him a distinct
and most enviable position among American authors. We of the
younger sort learn a lesson of reverent humility from the pure
enthusiasm with which he approaches and handles his noble themes.
The 'tone' of all his works is perfect. He is so thoroughly in sympathy with his subjects that the lay reader instantly shares his

feeling; and there is a kind of 'white light' pervading the whole—
prose and verse—which at any time tranquilizes and purifies the
mind."

The Rev. Robert Turnbull, D. D.:

"I have finished the reading of 'The Microcosm,' which has
afforded me unmingled delight. It is really a remarkable poem,
and has passages of great beauty and power. It cannot fail to
secure the admiration of all capable of appreciating it. Its ease,
its exquisite finish, its vivid yet delicate and powerful imagery, and
above all its sublime religious interest, entitle it to a very high place
in our literature."

John G. Whittier:

"Dr. Abraham Coles is a born hymn writer. No man living or
dead has so rendered the *text* and the *spirit* of the old and wonderful Latin Hymns. * * * His 'All the Days' and his 'Ever With
Thee' are immortal songs. It is better to have written them than
the stateliest of epics. * * * The idea of 'The Microcosm' is
novel and daring, but it is worked out with great skill and deli-
cacy. * * * 'The Evangel' is a work of piety and beauty. The
Proem opens with strong, vigorous yet melodious verse. I see no
reason why the Divine Story may not be fitly told in poetry."

Rev. S. I. Prime, D. D., in "The New York Observer":

"'The Evangel in Verse,' is the ripest fruit of the scholarship,
taste and poetic talent of one of our accomplished students of English verse, whose translations of 'Dies Iræ' and other poems have
made the name of Dr. Coles familiar in the literature of our day.
In the work before us he has attempted something higher and
better than any former essay of his skillful pen. He has rendered

the Gospel story of our Lord and Saviour into verse, with copious
notes, giving the largest amount of knowledge from critical
authorities to justify and explain the readings and to illuminate the
sacred narrative. . . . He excludes everything fictitious, and clings
to the orthodox view of the character and mission of the God-man.
The illustrations are a complete pictorial anthology. Thus the
poet, critic, commentator and artist has made a volume that will
take its place among the rare productions of the age, as an illustra-
tion of the genius, taste, and fertile scholarship of the author."

George Ripley, in the "New York Tribune":

"The purpose of this volume, 'The Evangel,' would be usually
regarded as beyond the scope of poetic composition. It aims to reproduce the scenes of the Gospel History in verse, with a strict adherence to the sacred narrative and no greater degree of imaginative
coloring than would serve to present the facts in the most brilliant
and impressive light. But the subject is one with which the author
cherishes so profound a sympathy, as in some sense to justify the
boldness of the attempt. The Oriental cast of his mind allures him
to the haunts of sacred song, and produces a vital communion with
the spirit of Hebrew poetry. Had he lived in the days of Isaiah or
Jeremiah, he might have been one of the bards who sought inspiration 'at Siloa's brook that flowed fast by the oracle of God.' The
present work is not the first fruits of his religious Muse, but he is
already known to the lovers of mediæval literature by his admirable translations of the 'Dies Iræ.' . . . The volume is brought out
in a style of unusual elegance, as it respects the essential requisites
of paper, print and binding, while the copious illustrations will attract notice by their selection of the most celebrated works of the
best masters."

The Rev. James McCosh, D. D., LL. D., upon the publication of "The Evangel:"

> "College of New Jersey,
>
> "PRINCETON, N. J.
>
> "You are giving to the world further proof that we did ourselves honor in conferring upon you some years ago the honorary degree of LL. D. * * * * I spent several hours last Sabbath in reading your poem, and relished it very much."

Daniel Haines (1801–1877), in 1843 elected Governor of New Jersey, and re-elected in 1847; Judge of the Supreme Court; one of the committee on the reunion of the two branches of the Presbyterian Church:

> "HAMBURG, N. J.
>
> "MY DEAR SIR—I can scarcely find fitting words in which to express my sincere thanks for your kind remembrance of me in the presentation of the beautiful copy of your recent work, 'The Evangel in Verse.' From the introduction, the proem and a few chapters, I judge it to be a work of rare excellence. The metrical composition is pleasant to the ear and eye, and is remarkable for its literal meaning. To me the greater charm is its clear and forcible expressions of evangelical truth and sound Christian doctrine.
>
> "It is the most succinct and complete refutation of the doctrine of Darwin and Huxley that I have seen.
>
> "The Christian most owes you a debt of gratitude for your labor and research, and heartfelt thanks to God for giving you the ability to produce a book so full of instruction, and affording so much gratification to the cultivated mind."

The Rev. George Dana Boardman, D. D.:

> " 'The Evangel in Verse' is a feast to the eye and ear and heart.

The careful exegesis, the conscientious loyalty to the statements of
the Holy Story, the sympathetic reproduction of a remote and
Oriental past, the sacred insight into the meaning of the Peerless
Career, the homageful yet manly, unsuperstitious reverence, the
rhythm as melodious as stately, the frequent notes, opulent in learning and doctrine and devotion, the illustrations deftly culled from
whatever is choice in ancient and modern art, these are some of
the many excellencies which give to ' The Evangel in Verse' an immortal beauty and worth, adding it as another coronet for Him on
whose brow are many diadems."

The Rev. Charles Hodge, D. D., LL. D. (1797-1878):

" I admire the skill which ' The Evangel' displays in investing
with rainbow hues the simple narrations of the Gospels. All, however, who have read Dr. Coles' versions of the ' Dies Iræ' and other
Latin Hymns must be prepared to receive any new productions
from his pen with high expectations. In these days when even the
clerical office seems in many cases insufficient to protect from the
present fashionable form of scepticism, it is a great satisfaction to
see a man of science and a scholar adhering so faithfully to the
simple Gospel."

The Hon. Frederick Theodore Frelinghuysen :

"United States Senate Chamber,

"WASHINGTON, D. C.

"MY DEAR DOCTOR—Many thanks to you for having written
'The Evangel.' It is admirably conceived and executed. While
the poem impresses the truth, it will lure many who would have
remained uninformed to the valuable instruction contained In the
Notes. The notes on Darwin, The Logos, Herod, and the miracle
at Ajalon, are excellent. The poem brings out many scriptural

truths, which are not on the surface.   Let me say, it is a great thing
to have written the book—to have your labor associated with salvation."

The Rev. Robert Lowell, D.D., in the "Church Monthly":

" Dr Coles is plainly a man of a very religious heart and a deeply
reverential mind. . . . Moreover he has so much learning in his
favorite subject, and so much critical instinct and experience, that
those who can relish honest thinking, and tender and most skillful
and true deductions, accept his teaching and suggestion with a ready
—sometimes surprised—sympathy and confidence.   Add to all this,
that he has the sure taste of a poet, and the warm and loving earn-
estness of a true believer in the redeeming Son of God, and the
catholic spirit of one who knows with mind and heart that Christianity at its beginning was Christianity, and we have the man who can
write such books as earnest Christian people will welcome and be
thankful for. . . . In this new book he proposes 'that ' The Evangel'
shall be a poetic version, and verse by verse paraphrase, so far as it
goes, of the Four Gospels, anciently and properly regarded as one.'
He makes an exquisite plea, in his preface, for giving leave to the
glad words to rejoice at the Lord's coming in the Flesh, for which all
other beings and things show their happiness. . . . . In the notes
the reader will find (if he have skill for such things) a treasure-house,
in which everything is worthy of its place.   Where he has offered
new interpretations, or set forth at large interpretations not generally received or familiar, he modestly asks only to have place given
him, and gives every one free leave to differ.   Everywhere there is
the largest and most true-hearted charity. . . . The reader cannot
open anywhere without finding in these notes, if he be not wiser or
more learned than ourselves, a great deal that he never saw, or
never saw so well set forth before."

Stephen Alexander, LL. D., Professor of Mechanics and Astronomy in the College of New Jersey:

"Princeton, N. J.

"Abraham Coles, M. D., LL. D.:

"My Dear Sir—I have delayed the acknowledgement of the receipt of your beautiful 'Evangel' until I could make some return after the same fashion. Please accept my sincere thanks, as well as my congratulations on your great success. I am always interested in your books, and always learn something from them.

"With this I send a copy of my 'Statement and Exposition of Certain Harmonies of the Solar System,' which I hope may reach you safely. Please accept the same, with my respects and regards. I think the Notes at the end and the supplement may especially interest you."

Dr. Oliver Wendell Holmes :

"There is a kind of straightforward simplicity about the poetical paraphrases which reminds one of the homelier but still always interesting verses which John Bunyon sprinkles like drops of heavenly dew along the pages of the Pilgrim's Progress. The illustrations add much to the work, in the way of ornament, and aid to the imag-ination. One among them is of terrible power, as it seems to me, such as it would be hard to show the equal of in the work of any modern artist. I mean Holman Hunt's 'Scapegoat.' There is a whole Theology in that picture. It haunts me with its fearful suggestiveness like a nightmare. I find 'The Evangel' an impressive and charming book. It does not provoke criticism—it is too devout, too sincere, too thoroughly conscientious in its elaboration to allow of fault-finding or fault-hunting."

William Cullen Bryant :

"I have read 'The Evangel' with pleasure and satisfaction. The

versification of the Lord's Prayer is both an expansion of the sense
and a commentary. The thought has often occurred to me what a
world of meaning is there wrapped up, and that meaning is admirably brought out."

Henry Woodhull Green, LL. D., (1802–1876), Chief
Justice of the Supreme Court of New Jersey from 1846
till 1860, when he became Chancellor:

"Trenton, N. J.

"Abraham Coles, LL. D., Newark, N. J.:

"My Dear Sir—I have read as much of 'The Evangel' during
the month since I received it as my leisure and the state of my
health have permitted. Of its literary merits, I do not feel myself
qualified to judge, but its perusal has given me great pleasure. I
have been particularly impressed with the fidelity with which you
have adhered to the sacred narrative, unmarred by the decorations
of heathen mythology or papal fable. I regard that as no ordinary
merit. I can well understand the strong temptation under which a
man of high classic culture must, in a work of this kind, constantly
labor, to turn from the stern simplicity of the sacred narrative to
seek embellishment amid the flowers of classic fiction. To have
resisted successfully such temptation, I regard as a very high merit;
and I congratulate you on the production of a work, which, I cannot
doubt, will redound to your own honor and the honor of our State.
With high regard, I am, very respectfully yours."

Charles H. Spurgeon, writing from Westwood, Beulah
Hill, Upper Norwood, speaks of "The Evangel" as "a
grand volume," and concludes his affectionate letter
with the words:

"Peace be to you, and every blessing. May Scotch Plains be a spot wherein Jesus dwells with a happy household. Yours very heartily."

The Hon. William Earl Dodge, (1805–1883), merchant and philanthropist, in a letter, written from his residence in New York City, to Dr. Coles:

"Mrs. Dodge and myself have very much enjoyed 'The Evangel,' having carefully read it. Such perfect conformity to the text and spirit of the sacred narrative, so beautifully transferred to verse, we have seldom found."

Thomas Gordon Hake, M. D., author of "Madeline, and Other Poems and Parables":

> "12 Portland place,
> "West Kensington, W., LONDON.

"I have read 'The Evangel,' and 'The Light of the World,' with deep interest, and with assurance that the learning and intelligence displayed in executing so difficult a work will secure it a lasting place in our joint national literature."

The "New York Observer":

"The skill of Dr. Coles as an artistic poet, his reverent, religious spirit, and the exalted flight of his muse in the regions of holy meditation are familiar to our readers. It is, therefore, superfluous for us to do more than announce a new and elegant volume from his pen—'The Microcosm and Other Poems.' It is rich in its contents. 'The Microcosm' is an essay in verse on the science of the human Body; it is literally the science of physiology condensed into 1,400 lines. The many occasional poems that follow are the efflorescence of a mind sensitive to the beautiful and rejoicing in the true; find-

ing God in everything, and delighting to trace the revelation of His
love in all the works of His hand. Such a volume is not to be
looked at for a moment and then laid aside. Like the great epics,
it is a book for all time, and will lose none of its interest and value
by the lapse of years. The publishers have given it a splendid dress,
and the illustrations add greatly to the attractions of this truly elegant book."

The "New York Times":

"The flavor of the book, 'The Microcosm and Other Poems,' is
most quaint, suggesting, on the religious side, George Herbert, and
on the naturalistic side, the elder Darwin, who, in 'The Botanic
Garden,' laid the seed of the revolution in science, accomplished by
the patient genius of his grandson. Some of the hymns for children
are beautiful in their simplicity and truth."

"The Critic":

"The long poem, 'The Microcosm,' which gives its name to the
present collection, has many beautiful and stately passages. Among
the shorter pieces following it, is to be found some of the best devo-
tional and patriotic poetry that has been written in this country."

John Y. Foster, author and editor, in "Frank Les-
lie's Illustrated Newspaper":

"In this exquisite and brilliantly illustrated volume, the scholarly
author has gathered up various children of his pen and grouped
them in family unity. 'The Microcosm,' which forms one-fifth of the
volume of 350 pages, is an attempt to present, in poetical form, a
compendium of the science of the human body. In originality of
conception and felicity of expression, it has not been approached by
any work of our best modern poets. The other poems are all
marked by the highest poetic taste, having passages of great beauty
and power."

Hon. Justin McCarthy :

"20 Cheyne Garden, Chelsea, LONDON, England.

"DEAR DR. COLES—I am surprised to see, in looking through your volume, 'The Microcosm and Other Poems,' that you have been able to add three more versions to those you have already made of that wonderful Latin hymn, perhaps the greatest of all, 'Dies Iræ.' Certainly it is one of the most difficult to translate. I like your last version especially."

The "Examiner and Chronicle":

"The title-poem in this exquisitely printed and charmingly illustrated volume, 'The Microcosm and Other Poems,' has been for some time before the public, and has received generous commendation for the tact and skill evinced in handling a very unpromising theme. A poetic description, minute and thorough going of the human body was a serious undertaking; but Dr. Coles delights in what is difficult and hazardous. He had already associated his name forever with the mediæval Latin hymn, 'Dies Iræ,' by publishing no less than thirteen distinct versions of it. In the volume before us he gives us three more versions. The other poems will not detract from the author's previous reputation."

Hon. Horace N. Congar, lawyer, editor, United States Consul at Hong Kong, China, under President Lincoln; and Consul at Prague, Bohemia, under President Grant:

"United States Consulate,

"PRAGUE, Bohemia.

"There is one thing, my dear Doctor, about your publications which no one can deny. You print your own poetical thoughts and conceptions. They are not copies of some other writer, but stand out clear and distinct with your own diction and strength; written for the scholarly and intelligent, they preserve true simplicity with the real grandeur of their conception."

The Rev. William Hague, D. D. (1808-1887), in "Life Notes; or Fifty Years' Outlook":

"The (Newark) 'Advertiser' yet lives and thrives, winning to its service the contributions of scholarly writers, among whom we have noticed, occasionally, the veteran physician and poet, Dr. Abraham Coles, author of 'The Evangel' with its immense wealth of critical scholasticism; and the tasteful and rhythmic translator of Latin poetry that enriches our libraries, for instance, in the artistically wrought edition of the 'Dies Iræ.'"

The "Newark Daily Advertiser":

"'The Microcosm' is the only book of the kind in the language, and is well deserving of a place in every library, and might, we think, moreover, be introduced with advantage into all *schools* where *physiology* is taught as an adjunct, if nothing else, to stimulate interest, and relieve the dryness of ordinary text books. In lines of flowing and easy verse, the author sets forth with a completeness certainly remarkable, and with great power and beauty the incomparable marvels of structure and function of the human body.

"This poetic mastery, making ductile the most unpromising materials, has had its latest and supreme exemplification in the completion of the unique work, 'The Life and Teachings of Our Lord, in Verse.' 'The Evangel,' forming the first part, appeared in 1874, 'The Light of the World,' forming the second part and completing the work, is now, 1884, first published. * * *

"By common consent the story of the life of Jesus, as told by the four evangelists, is the unmatched masterpiece of literature.

Its literary interest is hardly inferior to its religious. It is pre-emi
nently classic. The most fervid encomiums have come from infidels
and the great literary artists of the world. To taboo it, therefore,
as something outside of literature, betrays ignorance and imbecility.
Mr. Edwin Arnold has duly celebrated in his poem, 'The Light of
Asia,' the Buddhist hero, Prince Siddartha, and has had, it would
seem, readers among all classes. The life and teachings of Him
who is 'The Light of the World,' and whose fame fills the ages,
are surely not less worthy of regard and study by the cultiva-
tors of literature. The author has striven, it would seem, to make
his book a veritable cyclopædia of religious knowledge, so compre-
hensive is its scope. It ranges through the Old Testament and the
New. An episode in the first part, outlines nearly the whole history of the Jewish people. The poetical proem and the note appended thereto are in effective antagonism to Darwinism and cur-
rent evolution theories. An elaborate note on 'The Logos' gives
an historical summary of the prevailing creeds and christologies
from the earliest times.

"It is not too much to say that it is a book deserving of a place
beside the New Testament in every household, and cannot fail to
be found a valuable help to every reader and student of the sacred
Scriptures."

The Rev. George Dana Boardman, D. D.:

"Philadelphia, Pa.

"My Dear Doctor Coles—Most happy do I count myself in
possessing 'The Light of the World.' It has all those same fine
characteristics which so richly mark 'The Evangel.' It must be a
source of supreme delight to the accomplished author that he has
been permitted to complete a work so lofty in design, and so admirable in execution."

Rev. Alfred Spencer Patton, D. D. (1825–1888), author, editor of "The Baptist Weekly," etc.:

"Our good and gifted friend, Dr. Abraham Coles, has every reason to be gratified with the highly complimentary notices by the press, of his last work, 'The Light of the World,' it being the second volume or completion of his life of Jesus, as told by the evangelists."

The Hon. Joseph P. Bradley, LL. D., one of the Justices of the Supreme Court of the United States :

"WASHINGTON, D. C., Dec. 14, 1884.

"DEAR DOCTOR—I have read nearly all of your beautiful book, 'The Life and Teachings of Our Lord, in Verse,' and like it better the longer I read it. You had two rocks to avoid: on one side *prosaic tameness*, which might be incurred by too rigid an adherence to the text; on the other *rashness* in attempting (even poetical) changes of consecrated forms of expression—changes which no English or American ear would endure. I appreciate the difficulty of the task, and think you have performed it wonderfully well."

John G. Whittier:

"AMESBURY, Mass., January, 1885.

" 'The Light of the World' I have read with interest. Thy poetical version of the wonderful narrative seems to be conscientiously faithful to the original, while at the same time it successfully interprets some passages which are not clear to the ordinary reader. It will be a helpful book to many, who will realize, for the first time, the true meaning and significance of the Lord's words. I am, with high respect and esteem, thy friend."

The Right Honorable John Bright, M. P., England:

"132 Picadilly, London, April 30, 1885.

"Dear Dr. Coles—When I began to read your volume on 'The Life and Teachings of Christ in Verse,' I thought you had attempted to gild the refined gold, and would fail—as I proceeded in my reading that idea gradually disappeared, and I discovered that you had brought the refined gold together in a manner convenient and useful and deeply interesting. I have read the volume with all its notes, many of which seem to me of great value. I could envy you the learning and the industry that have enabled you to produce this remarkable work. I hope it may have many readers in all countries where our language is spoken."

The Rev. Henry Griggs Weston, D. D., author and editor, President of the Crozer Theological Seminary, Chester, Pennsylvania:

"Your work, 'The Life and Teachings of Our Lord,' is one of the gratifying fruits of the study which the Gospels have received since I first began to inquire for helps to their understanding."

The Rev. Horatius Bonar, D. D.:

"10 Palmerston Road, Grange, Edinburgh.

* * * * "I am struck with your command of language, and your skill in clothing the simplicities of history with the elegance of poetry. It ('The Life and Teachings of Our Lord in Verse') is no ordinary volume, and your notes are of a very high order indeed—admirably written, and full of philosophical thought and Scriptural research."

The Rev. Alexander McLaren, D. D.:

" MANCHESTER, Eng., Nov. 3, 1885.

"DEAR SIR—I congratulate you on having accomplished with such success a most difficult undertaking; and on having been able to present the inexhaustible life in a form so new and original. I do not know whether I have been most struck by the careful and fine exegetical study, or the graceful versification of your work. I trust it ('The Life and Teachings of Our Lord in Verse') may be useful, not only in attracting the people, which George Herbert thought could be caught with a song, when they would run from a sermon, but may also help lovers of the sermon to see its subject in a new garb."

Adele M. Fielde, missionary at Swatow, China :

" Those whose judgment is of value have given Dr. Coles' translations of the Latin hymns such high praise, that words of commendation from me would appear presumptuous. I am glad, for the world's sake, that the wonderful Latin hymns were written, and that Dr. Coles has so translated them, and I am glad for my own sake that I have them to read. * * * * I think Dr. Coles has done an excellent thing for us in his 'Life and Teachings of Our Lord.' "

Elizabeth Clementine Kinney, author and poet, wife of Hon. William Burnet Kinney; and, by her first husband, Edmund B. Stedman, the mother of Edmund Clarence Stedman, the distinguished poet and critic :

" Dr. Coles long ago established a high reputation in both worlds, by his matchless translations of that famous old judgment hymn, the 'Dies Iræ,' and of mediæval hymns, published under the title of 'Old Gems in New Settings;' also by his unique original poem,

'The Microcosm,' which has glorified by immortal verse this mortal body, so fearfully and wonderfully made that every part harmonizes with the poet's song. In 'The Evangel' and 'The Light of the World,' already noticed by 'The Observer,' while conscientiously adhering to the sacred text, Dr. Coles' frequent elaborate notes give freedom to some original suggestions growing out of the author's fifty years' devout study of the Bible. It will be well to heed any proposition brought forward by one who has been so long a reverent student as to have become a profound thinker, and thus an able teacher of the divine word. Every thought or idea advanced by Dr. Coles will, doubtless, on thorough, unprejudiced investigation, be found supported by a reasonable interpretation of Scripture. Between the acts of this sacred drama there are also some hymnal excursions, which show the height and depth, the color and light, the melody and ecstasy, of the true Christian poet. Through his many works, one noble aim is ever apparent, viz.: to 'crown Him Lord of all' who is 'the author and finisher of our faith' and 'the giver of every good and perfect gift.' Noticeable, too, through all, is progression, in respect of enlargement by study and thought; of advancement with advancing years, keeping pace with the age in increasing light so far as it develops heavenly truth, and original conception through truth."

"The Book Buyer," Charles Scribner's Sons, New York:

"'The Hebrew Psalms in English Verse.' By Abraham Coles, M. D., LL. D. Dr. Coles has won praise from some of the most eminent of critics for his translations into English of the 'Dies Iræ,' the characteristics of the work being faithfulness to the spirit of the original, combined with a command of rich and rythmic English. His tastes have led him to translate the great Hebrew classic into English verse, a task of unusual difficulty which many have

undertaken, but in which few have attained even partial success.
Dr. Coles's work will attract wide attention by reason of its lofty religious spirit, its admirable reflection of the incomparably fine flavor
of the original, its dignified, stately diction and the scholarly care
bestowed upon every line. The book, moreover, has an additional
value in the prefatory matter which includes an essay on the character of the Psalms, a detailed account of the French, English and
Scotch metrical versions of the Psalms and a chapter of interesting
notes, critical, historical and biographical. An admirable steel
portrait of Dr. Coles serves as a frontispiece to the book."

Rev. Theodore L. Cuyler, D. D., LL. D.:

"DEAR DR. COLES—Your volume on the Psalms is a noble work,
and the introduction is rich and sweet as a honeycomb. Two Sabbaths ago I gave out from my pulpit your fine hymn, 'Lo, I am with
you all the days,' and told the congregation some things about the
author. * * * * You will be quite at home up among heaven's
choir of psalmists and chosen singers."

The "New York Tribune":

"'A New Rendering of the Hebrew Psalms into English Verse,
with Notes, Critical, Historical and Biographical, including an
Historical Sketch of the French, English and Scotch Metrical
Versions,' by Dr. Abraham Coles. Dr. Coles' name on the
title-page is a sufficient indication of the excellence and thorough-
ness of the work done. Indeed, Dr. Coles has done much more
than produce a fresh, vigorous and harmonious version of the
Psalms, though this was alone well worth doing. His full and scholarly notes on the early versions of Clement Marot, Sternhold and
Hopkins and others, his sketches of eminent persons connected in
various ways with particular psalms, his literary and bibliographical

information, together impart a value and interest to this work which should insure an extensive circulation for it. Very much of the historical and other matter thus brought within the reach of the public is inaccessible to such as have not means of access to public libraries, and there is certainly no Christian household in the country which would not find both pleasure and instruction in Dr. Coles' compendious and altogether unique volume. It may be added that in his version of the Psalms he has wisely preserved the rhythmical swing and the terse language which distinguish the early renderings, and that therefore those who have been reared on the old versions need not fear finding their favorites changed 'out of knowledge.'"

The Rev. Frederic W. Farrar, D. D., F. R. S., Chaplain in Ordinary to the Queen, author of the "Life of Christ," etc., in a letter to Dr. Coles:

"17, Dean's Yard, WESTMINSTER, S. W.

"The task of versifying the Psalms was too much even for Milton, but you have attempted it with seriousness and with as much success as seems to be possible. I was much interested in your introduction."

The Rev. A. H. Tuttle, D. D., pastor of the First Methodist Episcopal Church, Wilkesbarre, Pa.:

"'The Life and Teachings of Our Lord, in verse,' has greatly aided me in my efforts to interpret heavenly things. I am glad you have lived to complete your versification of the Psalms. I am now making a protracted and careful study of the old Hebrew Hymn Book, and your work will be of untold help to me. I have already read my favorite psalms as you sing them. They are rich beyond expression."

The Rev. Charles S. Robinson, D. D.:

"I have read many of your really excellent versions of the Psalms. It seems to me you have added richly to our available literature in that direction. I have been specially interested, also, in the prefaced notes. Some of the information is quite new to me, and the comments are all good and helpful."

Hon. George Hay Stuart, the eminent philanthropist in January, 1888, wrote from Philadelphia:

"'The New Rendering of the Hebrew Psalms into English Verse,' I prize very much. It is exceedingly good and very suggestive. The subject matter is of peculiar interest to me. I have been brought up, as perhaps you know, in old Rouse's version of the Psalms, but never held the view, that many do, that nothing else can be sung in the praise of God. Our own congregation, up to recently, used nothing but that version. Now we have so far advanced that we sing, also, hymns and spiritual songs. * * * * The United Presbyterian Assembly has recently adopted a new version of the Psalms, but I think their leading men ought to see this version."

The Rev. D. R. Frazer, D. D., pastor of the First Presbyterian Church, of Newark, N. J.:

"MY DEAR DR. COLES—I do not know that I can give any better expression of my appreciation of your last work than to say that my wife and I sat up until after midnight, reading psalm after psalm with very great delight. The versification is beautiful, and its beauty intensifies by its fidelity to the common version. Hoping the book may do much good, in making manifest the beauties of one of the most beautiful portions of the Word of God, I am, with great respect, ever sincerely yours."

Charles M. Davis, Secretary of the American Institute of Christian Philosophy, Superintendent of Public Schools, Essex county, N. J., etc.:

"Dear Dr. Coles—During the past year I have been reading the revised version of the Psalms, in connection with the received. Your translations will be a help to me, as I do not understand Hebrew. I have read your introduction very carefully, and find it contains especially valuable information, as do, also, your occasional notes. The psalms that I have read aloud in the family have been greatly enjoyed, especially the 107th, 136th and 137th. We are anticipating much pleasure from the continuance of this during the winter evenings."

The Rev. A. H. Lewis, D. D., editor of "The Outlook and Sabbath Quarterly":

"I have been greatly interested in the book, not only in the success which you have attained in versifying the Psalms, but in the valuable matter embodied in the introduction. I have usually found it difficult to interest myself in any versification of the Psalms, especially in the early efforts by Watts and others. On opening your volume, I found myself inclined to read in detail, rather than to examine cursorily. It is very difficult to versify Hebrew poetry. The success you have attained in expressing the delicate shades of sentiment commands our congratulations, and may justly give you abundant satisfaction."

S. W. Kershaw, F. S. A., author, librarian of the Lambeth Palace Library, London, England, etc.:

"Lambeth Library, 12 June, 1888.

"* * * * In this library there is a fine collection of works on the liturgies, prayer-book, etc. In your 'New Rendering of the

Hebrew Psalms Into English Verse,' I am greatly interested in the introduction, in reading about the psalms of Clement Marot, and in the allusion to the Huguenots.   My little book on the 'Protestants from France in their English home' was kindly reviewed in one of your papers. * * * *"

J. K. Hoyt, editor and author:

"BAY VIEW, Florida.

"DEAR DR. COLES—I have passed a very pleasant Sunday morning in looking over your new book. I wish you had invoked the spirit of Beethoven, and written the music as well as the words; for the proper use of a metrical version of the Psalms is to sing them. Still, the book is a wonderful one, and encourages me to believe that age is not necessarily a bar to work.   I enjoy the notes much, and very often find myself turning from the essay to the verses referred to.   You will leave a melodious monument behind you, my good Doctor."

The Rev. George Dana Boardman, D. D.:

"MY DEAR DR. COLES—I greatly admire your new book for many reasons : first, for its rich introduction, felicitously describing the character of the Psalms, giving us an exhaustive history of metrical versions, presenting critical, historical and biographical notes of great value ; secondly, for your new rendering of the Psalms, a rendering conscientious, mellifluous, fresh and suggestive; thirdly, and not least, for the frontispiece, representing one who has both the David spirit and the David music.   Faithfully yours."

The Rev. Lewis R. Dunn, D. D.:

"I like the 'rhythmic flow' of the words of your work, its truths,
its thorough orthodoxy, its blending of the results of most recent
scholarship in lines and notes, its beautiful illustrations of the text,
and its high intellectual and spiritual tone—a classic in our good
old English tongue."

Asahel Clark Kendrick, D. D., LL. D., author, Professor of Hebrew, Greek and Latin in the University of
Rochester, New York:

"In your translation of the Hebrew Psalms into English verse,
you may well be congratulated in having thus nobly crowned
your series of poems devoted to those themes, which aid the aspirations of the soul upward toward God and heaven, and may well
task the highest human efforts. The renderings are in clear
and weighty verse, fitted to the noble simplicity of the original; and
the notes are instructive and valuable."

George MacDonald, author and poet:

"LONDON, England.

"MY DEAR DOCTOR COLES.—I send you by this post a copy of
my little book on the religious poetry of England. I am sure you
will find a good deal to sympathize with in it. * * * I am sorry
to say I have not yet received your book, which I should like much
to see after the taste you gave me, sheltered and ministered unto
by you and yours. Let me hope I may once more be your guest,
and that you may be ours. Believe in my love and gratitude.
Yours, with sincere affection."

The Rev. Philip Schaff, D. D., LL. D., in " Literature
and Poetry," Charles Scribner's Sons, New York, 1890 :

" A physician, Abraham Coles, prepared between 1847 and 1859
thirteen versions (of the ' Dies Iræ '), six of which are in the trochaic
measure and double rhyme of the original, five in the same rhythm,
but in single rhyme, one in iambic triplets, like Roscommon's, the
last in quatrains, like Crashaw's version. Two appeared anony-
mously in the Newark ' Daily Advertiser,' the first one in 1847,
and a part of it found its way into Mrs. Stowe's ' Uncle Tom's
Cabin ; ' subsequently this version was set to music in Henry
Ward Beecher's ' Plymouth Collection of Hymns and Tunes.'
The thirteen versions were first published together with an introduction in 1859. He has since published three additional versions in double rhyme, New York, 1881, in ' The Microcosm and
Other Poems.' In August, 1889, he made one more version in
single rhyme and four lines. These seventeen versions show a
rare fertility and versatility, and illustrate the possibilities of
variation, without altering the sense. Dr. Coles, in the eleventh
stanza of his first translation of 1847, had anticipated Irons,
Périès, and Dix:

> " ' Righteous Judge of retribution,
> Make me gift of absolution
> Ere that day of execution.'

* * * " Dr. Abraham Coles, of Scotch Plains, N. J., the successful translator of ' Dies Iræ,' and ' Stabat Mater,' has reproduced,
but has not yet (1889), published, all the passion hymns of St.
Bernard."